BEHIND CLOSED DOORS

By Kimberla Lawson Roby

Too Much of a Good Thing
A Taste of Reality
It's a Thin Line
Casting the First Stone
Here and Now
Behind Closed Doors

Coming Soon in Hardcover

The Best-Kept Secret

BEHIND CLOSED DOORS

Kimberla Lawson Roby

AVON
TRADE

An Imprint of HarperCollins*Publishers*

This book was originally published by Lenox Press and Black Classics Press in 1997.

Excerpt from *Too Much of a Good Thing* copyright © 2004 by Kimberla Lawson Roby.

HarperCollins books may be purchased for education, business, or sales promotional use. For information please write: Special Markets Department, HarperCollins Publishers Inc., 10 East 53rd Street, New York, NY 10022.

FIRST EDITION

Designed by Elizabeth M. Glover

The 1997 trade paperback edition contains the following Library of Congress Cataloging-in-Publication Data

Roby, Kimberla Lawson
    Behind closed doors / Kimberla Lawson Roby

1. Women—United States—Fiction. 2. Afro-American Women—Fiction. I. Title.

96-94608

    05 06 07 08 JTC/RRD 10 9 8 7 6

In memory of my maternal grandparents,
Clifton Sr. and Mary Tennin

Acknowledgments

At this point, God has blessed me to write seven books. But *Behind Closed Doors* will *always* be my baby. It is the first book I ever wrote and the book that began my career as a novelist. It is the book my mom and husband believed in from the very beginning—even though I wasn't so sure what the feedback from others would be.

But as it turned out, *Behind Closed Doors* quickly became a Blackboard and Essence best seller. Partly because of all the wonderfully dedicated readers who gave it a chance and partly because of Emma Rodgers, owner of Black Images Book Bazaar in Dallas, Texas. This amazing woman immediately called *Behind Closed Doors* her baby and encouraged every one of her customers to purchase it. And if that wasn't enough, she phoned other independent bookstores and encouraged them to order and sell it. So, from the bottom of my heart, Emma, I

ACKNOWLEDGMENTS

thank you. Additionally, I am thankful to Frances Utsey at The Cultural Connection Bookstore in Milwaukee, who also hand-sold copy after copy.

I'd also like to thank every individual who supported me from the moment *Behind Closed Doors* was first released in January 1997: my wonderful husband, Will M. Roby Jr.; my mother, Arletha Stapleton, who is now deceased but is still very much with me; my brothers, Willie Jr. and Michael Stapleton; my dearest friends and supporters, Lori Whitaker Thurman, Kelli Tunson Bullard, Janell Green, Aileen Blacknell, Veronda Johnson, Dorothy Wright, Shurice Hunter, Christine Williams, Keith and Shari Grace of Grace Design, Paul Coates and Apryl Motley at Black Classic Press, Martha Moore, Mary Carthell, Vicky Pruitt, and Barb Polster. Thank you all for having such confidence in me from the start.

Many thanks to Carolyn Marino, Jennifer Civiletto, Michael Morrison, Lisa Gallagher, Debbie Stier and everyone else at HarperCollins for producing this new edition. It's a dream come true.

And to my readers, thank you for your continued support. I am indebted.

CHAPTER 1

REGINA CRUISED the silver Mercedes in front of her two-story house and beamed with much admiration. The mere sight of Wesleyan Estates sent chills through her entire body. Perfectly landscaped lawns, a nearby golf course, gorgeous houses occupied by wealthy residents. She'd been blessed. Blessed at the age of thirty with what most black people were never able to reap throughout an entire lifetime. And it had all transpired in such perfect order too, one splendid event right after another. Graduating from U of I with no preposterous student loan balances to repay, marrying a well-educated, highly paid, gorgeous-looking black man named Larry, and then purchasing this immaculate home, located in a ninety-nine-percent white, upper-echelon subdivision. Simply put, they had it all. They'd obtained the American dream without even realizing it.

She crept past Larry's crystal white Lexus, parked next to the Cherokee inside the two-car garage, and frowned when she realized the door had been left wide open. She'd fussed at Larry no less than a thousand times for not closing that garage door, and still he didn't seem to be paying her the slightest bit of attention. Just didn't seem to be worried, since they lived in this ritzy neighborhood. But then he'd have a totally different attitude once all of those expensive yard toys of his came up missing. That high-tech electric edger, top-of-the-line snow thrower, and brand-new mulching lawn mower. It was so strange how men always had to learn everything the hard way. Just couldn't tell them anything.

She removed the key from the ignition, stepped out of the car, shut the door, pressed the garage door control on the wall, and walked through the door leading to the hunter green, country-style kitchen. She spotted today's mail stacked on the wooden, tiled-top table where Larry had left it. Bills, bills, bills. Not a day seemed to pass by without one showing up. Nordstrom, Saks, Visa, Discover. She might as well have listed them as joint owners on her checking account with all the checks that were written out to each of them every month, she thought, tossing the bills back onto the table one by one. But at the bottom of the pile was an elegant picture of Oprah Winfrey displayed across the cover of *Essence* magazine. It was their twenty-fifth anniversary issue, and it appeared to be pretty interesting. She'd definitely have to make sure and find time to read this before the weekend was over.

As she climbed the winding stairs and entered the up-stairs hallway, she heard the shower running. It was a bit early to be getting ready for a nine o'clock show, the one she and Larry usually took in every Friday night, but maybe he'd decided to take her to a real restaurant for a change and not one of those tasteless fast-food places. She was sick of eating generic seafood every Friday night. The Boston Sea Party was far more to her liking, and that's where she prayed they were going.

Regina walked into the master bedroom, kicked off her navy blue pumps, slipped out of the navy blue crepe suit and carefully removed her panty hose by Christian Dior. Yesterday, before the clock in her office had barely struck noon, she'd torn a gigantic run in the ones she'd been wearing, and she was planning to get at least one or two more wears out of this pair before having to pitch them in the wastebasket. She'd known for a long time that these things were way too expensive, but as far as she was concerned, the ones they sold in some of those discount stores never seemed to cut it.

She heard the water tapering off and the shower door slide open. "Hey, hon," Regina said, walking into the bath-room, shedding her underwear. "How was your day?"

Larry stepped out of the shower, sawing his back with a burgundy velvet bath towel. "It was okay. How was yours?"

Regina leaned over and pecked him on the lips. "It was a typical Friday, but I'm glad the weekend has final-ly gotten here. It was a long week."

Larry finished drying himself off, moved in front of the double mirror, picked up his blue plastic razor, and began edging his mustache. "I know what you mean. It was a long week for me as well. I don't know when I've had so many meetings and so many insurance claims to review. Oh, by the way, Ted and I are going out to his boss's house again to play poker. Shouldn't be gone too late, though. I hope you don't mind."

Where did that shit come from? He hadn't mentioned going anywhere when she'd spoken with him at work. She'd assumed this Friday evening would be no different than any other. They would go to dinner, see a movie, and make love like two wild animals when they returned home. He had gone to play cards each of the two previous Fridays, but this once-every-week thing was a little more than she was willing to put up with, and it was starting to piss her off.

Regina placed her right hand on her hip, the way black women do when they intend to get their point across. "And what am I supposed to do sitting here all by myself on a Friday evening? This is the third week in a row. Here I am thinking you're about to take me out to a nice restaurant, and you're in here getting ready to hang out with Ted. We haven't gone anywhere together in two weeks, and I'm getting sick of this."

"We can go to the movies tomorrow. Right?"

"Do I have a choice? It sounds to me like you've already made your plans for the evening anyway," she said, staring straight at him.

4

Larry rinsed off the razor, then his face. "Look, Regina. Ever since we started dating three years ago, I've pretty much spent every single Friday evening with you, so why is it such a crime for me to go play cards one night a week? I don't see why you're making such a big deal out of this."

Regina was puzzled, but she had to admit that he was right. At least for the most part, because he had pretty much spent every Friday night with her since the day they'd gotten married. The only problem was, she didn't see anything wrong with it continuing. They were married, and that was what married people did. Spend time together. Not go their separate ways like two single individuals with no ties to each other. If he wanted to hang out with his unmarried friends and play the little bachelor role, then he should have never asked her to marry him. He'd had no problem with spending all of his time with her before, and she couldn't help but wonder what was going on now. Come to think of it, he'd been canceling their lunch dates as well, claiming he had too much work to do and then working an unusual amount of overtime in the evenings and on the weekends. Maybe he was starting to feel caught up. Maybe he needed his freedom to do whatever he wanted. Maybe he longed to be with someone else. They'd only been married two years, but hell, he was acting like he already had the seven-year itch and needed a nice, long scratch. Hmmph. Right now, she felt like giving it to him.

But Regina knew her imagination was working overtime, because with the exception of Larry leaving his clothes lying around for her to pick up, he was a good husband and a wonderful provider. She told herself he was only playing cards, and probably just wanted to do that male bonding thing that most men claimed they needed to do. Her secretary's husband hooked up with his friends every Thursday for what he called a "guys' night out," so what was wrong with Larry wanting to go out every now and then with Ted? The answer was obvious: absolutely nothing. She didn't know why she was being so silly.

"I don't see anything wrong with you going out every now and then, but it's just that I've sat at home alone for two Friday nights straight, and I'm really disappointed. I just wish you had told me earlier, so I wouldn't have gotten my heart set on spending some time with you."

"We'll do something tomorrow. I promise." He dried his face and kissed her on the forehead as he walked out of the bathroom.

Regina presented him with a bogus smile, stepped into the shower, and turned it on. The soothing, hot water running across her body felt so relaxing that she stood there for five whole minutes with no display of movement. She wished it would never end, but she could already feel the water slowly starting to cool down. There was only so much hot water available when she and Larry took long, steamy showers one right after the other.

Regina shut off the water and reached for her coral

pink bath towel. She walked out into the bedroom, dried most of her body off, and saw Larry putting on his dark olive dress pants and silk sweater. Clothing that was perfect for springtime weather, but inappropriate and too dressy if all he was going to do was play poker. Still though, as much as she hated to admit it, he was looking especially fine tonight. But then why shouldn't he? Whether it was a business suit for work or a pair of jeans for running around on the weekend, she always got him the very best that their hard-earned money could buy. This man's wardrobe had been a complete mess when they'd first gotten together, and it was obvious that he'd barely even heard of Marshall Field's, Saks, or Nordstrom, let alone purchased any clothing from any one of them. Back then, he'd been the cheapest man she'd met, and to tell the truth, he still was right now.

Larry had a high-yellow complexion, almost-black hair, grayish-brown eyes, and a perfect, athletic build. He was the ideal man for Regina, her being partial to light-skinned men and all, and by far the best-looking man she'd ever laid eyes on. Simply put, the man was finer than expensive wine, and it was no wonder that when she'd first met him, there had been at least a dozen female vultures trying hard to sink their vicious claws into him and the reason she'd gone to major extremes to make sure they hadn't come close to succeeding.

"You look nice," Regina said, wrapping the towel around her body and securing both ends together at the point just above her breasts.

"Thanks, baby."

Regina sat down on the side of the bed and watched him spray what must have been the last of his Cool Water cologne; just yesterday he'd asked her to pick him up a new bottle the next time she went to the mall. She crossed her legs and leaned back with both of her palms pressed against the bed. "What time will you be back?"

"Probably around nine or so. I'll call you if it gets to be later than that, though."

Uh-oh. She didn't like the sound of that. Last week, it had been after eleven when he'd finally remembered where home was, and she sure hoped he wasn't planning to stay out that late again.

Larry walked over to Regina, drew her into his arms, kissed her, and looked her straight in her caramel brown eyes. "I love you, baby, and I promise, we'll do whatever you want tomorrow."

"Have a good time," Regina said. She really didn't mean it, but she was trying to be sensible about this whole thing.

"I'll see you when I get back," Larry said and headed down the stairs.

Regina was about to follow him when she heard the phone ring. She answered it. "Hello?"

There was no answer.

"Hello? Hello?" Regina slammed the receiver on the hook and grunted. Nothing angered her more than when someone called and hung up. If a person had the wrong number, the very least they could do was apologize before simply hanging up in someone's ear.

"Who was that on the phone?" Larry yelled back up the stairs.

"Nobody important, I guess. They wouldn't say anything."

She heard him shut the kitchen door, and, not too long after, she heard the garage door closing. She couldn't believe it. He had actually remembered to shut it this time. Maybe there was hope for Larry Moore yet.

As REGINA reached for the remote control to switch the solid oak console TV to channel nine for the lottery results, the phone rang. She picked up the black cordless phone in the family room and pressed the Talk button. "Hello?"

No answer.

"Hello? Hello?"

There was still no response. Regina pursed her lips together, pressed the Talk button again, and slung the phone across the blue leather love seat. She was starting to get a little irritated with all of these hang-ups. They had become more and more frequent over the last month or so, and neither she nor Larry had the slightest idea who it could be. But this was finally it. She was calling Ameritech first thing Monday morning to order that Caller ID box that her best friend, Karen, had made such a fuss over and purchased just a few months ago. She had practically begged Regina to order one, and right now, Regina could kick herself for not doing it. "You spend money on everything else. Why not this?" Karen had asked. Regina had known Karen was right, but usually when she bought things she didn't need they were personal items like clothing, jewelry, shoes, or cosmetics— items for herself, not the general household. But now, though, this whole thing was getting out of hand, and she was starting to realize what a major relief it would be to find out who this unidentified caller was, and, more importantly, why he or she was calling in the first place.

The WGN announcer called out the Pick Four and Little Lotto numbers, and Regina jotted them down. 3-2-5-7 and 1-14-17-21-30. Whoever had made that phone call needed the crap beat out of them. Sister had missed the three digit, and nobody made her do that without hearing about it. Six months ago, Larry had yelled for her to come rinse out the relaxing cream from one of those wave curl kits he'd combed into his hair, explaining that it had been in for over twenty minutes and was slowly starting to burn his overly sensitive scalp. But Regina had ignored him and not moved one inch until the last of those lottery results had been flashed across the screen. By the time she'd made it down the stairs, Larry was trying ferociously to wash it out himself. Unfortunately for him, it was too late. Larry's babylike scalp was on fire, and within three days, sores had scattered about his entire head. Needless to say, he'd never interrupted Regina's Illinois lottery results again.

She reached over the left arm of the love seat, picked up her tan and evergreen shoulder bag, and pulled out the numbers she'd played at the 7-Eleven right after work. She checked the numbers twice but found that she hadn't matched one number. The outcome was no different than any of the other times she'd played, but as usual, a look of disappointment covered her face when she realized her numbers were nowhere in the proximity of the ones that had been drawn.

She gazed down at her watch and saw that it was nine-thirty. Larry still wasn't back yet. Hadn't even called, for that matter. He was being inconsiderate again, and she didn't appreciate this shit one bit. She was trying to understand, but damn, this man was trying her patience.

She stood up and walked toward the kitchen. She was hungry but too lazy to cook and unwilling to drive to some fast-food joint. The Chinese rice they'd picked up from Wong Wong last night was going to have to do. She pulled open the right door of the refrigerator, took out the small white box, emptied the rice onto a Tupperware plate, and centered it inside the microwave. She was never sure how long to set the timer for, but she settled on four minutes.

When the buzzer sounded, she removed the plate, took a fork from the drawer, and went back into the family room. She took one mouthful and felt a burning sensation dash across her tongue. "Goodness." It was way too hot. She sat the plate down on the floor to allow it some additional time to cool off.

After flipping through *TV Guide* and reading a few of
the articles, Regina checked to see if her food had fi-
nally cooled down. She picked up the remote control
and scanned through the channels. As usual, nothing
was on, so she turned off the TV. She finished the rice,
which she couldn't taste now that her tongue was
numb, stood up, walked over to the floor lamp, turned
it off, and left the family room. She wasn't in the mood
for washing any dishes, and two small items weren't
nearly enough to be loading into the dishwasher, so she
went into the kitchen, placed the fork and plate in the
sink, and headed upstairs.

In the bedroom, she moved toward the purple chaise
and lifted the suit she'd laid there right before taking a
shower. This one was her favorite. Partly because of the
gold buttons down the front, but mainly because it was a
size ten, and the waistband of the skirt no longer cut her
circulation off.

She was five foot six and not much on the heavy side,
but over the past two years, she had put on five or six un-
wanted pounds straight through her midsection.
Blaming it on being happily married and settled down.
But four months ago, when she'd become completely fed
up and hadn't seen any other way to shed this dreadful
weight, she'd persuaded Karen and her other good
friend, Marilyn, to sign up for a Saturday morning aero-
bics class at the health club, and she'd eventually per-
suaded them to start working out with the toning
machines two nights during the week. That is, until

about three weeks ago, when Karen had started missing the class and each of the weeknight toning sessions. Tomorrow, though, Regina was going to call her bright and early, because it was already mid-April, and she surely did not want to hear Karen complaining about all the weight she'd picked up over the winter and how hard it was going to be for her to lose it before the break of summer, which was barely two months away.

After hanging up her suit, Regina left the walk-in closet, went to the cherrywood king-size bed, and turned back the comforter. She sat down on the side and slipped off the Bulls T-shirt and black shorts she'd thrown on right after Larry had left. She debated as to whether she should slip on an everyday nightgown or take another shower and put on a sexy negligee. There was always the chance Larry would want to make love to her when he got home, and she wanted to be fresh. Of course, he hadn't made any attempts the two previous Fridays when he'd finally arrived, but it was better to be ready anyway, just in case he wanted her tonight.

When she stepped out of the shower, she dried off for the second time, sat on the edge of the tub, and lotioned her body. That peach-scented shower gel by Victoria's Secret smelled better than it had in the store, and she was going to make sure and stock up on it the next time she shopped at Woodfield Mall.

Regina was a beautiful woman. Her hair was perfectly cut in a short, faded style, similar to Anita Baker's, but with a wavier texture to it. The color was a sandy brown, which complimented her light complexion—a complexion that had her convinced that being light-skinned proved she was just a little more attractive than any and every dark-skinned sister in existence. Celebrities, supermodels. It didn't matter who they were or how gorgeous they looked. As far as she was concerned, the only competition she had when it came to beauty were other fairskinned black women or women who were white. Which was why it had always bothered her when men seemed to direct their attention toward Karen whenever they went out to a club. Karen was dark-skinned, and it just didn't make any sense. They would consistently ask Karen if she wanted to dance, if they could give her a call, or if they could take her to dinner. It had been that way all through college, and, quite honestly, not much different now that they were married. For the life of her, Regina couldn't understand it. She just couldn't see it.

Regina walked back into the bedroom, slipped on her black silk, above-the-knee nightgown, climbed into bed, and reached toward her nightstand to pick up Terry McMillan's *Waiting to Exhale*. She had already finished two other contemporary novels that she'd purchased a month ago, but last week, she had decided to read this one again. She, of course, didn't have any problems with finding or keeping a man the way the women in the book did, but she had still been thoroughly entertained by it.

She leaned back on two down-filled pillows, stretched her legs out under the covers, and glanced over at the clock on the VCR. It was pushing close to eleven o'clock, and still no Larry. Where the hell was he? This mess was getting out of hand, and she couldn't help but wonder what tired excuse he was going to conjure up this time. Damn him.

CHAPTER 2

KAREN RAISED UP on her side of the bed and glanced over at the brightly lit alarm clock. It was midnight, and John still wasn't home yet. *Damn*, she thought. *He must have his obsessive ass at that horse track again.* Every Friday for the last two months, John had blundered and found his way to the horse track, where he'd blown practically every single dime of his paycheck. And today would be no different. Apparently, the Illinois State lottery just wasn't enough for him anymore. Of course, she'd never approved of that either, but at least when he played the lottery, he wasn't spending their bill money.

Karen was getting fed up, and she was going to put an end to all of this nonsense as soon as he brought his compulsive ass through that back door. John had blown so much money this month that she'd been forced to withdraw funds from her employee credit union account to cover bills their paychecks should have easily satisfied. This was plain asinine, and she'd decided tonight that although they had a great marriage, she'd be by herself before she would let a trifling-ass gambler take her to the poorhouse. She simply wasn't going to have this mess.

Karen noticed a light flash through the master bedroom window and thought maybe it was John. She hopped up, marched over to the window, and peeped through one of the slats of the left mini-blind. But when she looked down at the driveway, all she saw was a smaller car pull in, back out, and then drive back toward the entrance of Ridgemore East's subdivision. People were always using their driveway to redirect themselves when they had lost their way, and that was one of the main reasons she had despised purchasing a house on a cul-de-sac.

Karen was more pissed off now than before. Here she was hightailing it to the window like a chicken with its head cut off while John was out practically tossing their money away.

She tarried her tall, five-foot-nine-and-a-half-inch body across the light tan, plush carpet of the master bedroom and switched on the ceiling fan. As she passed by the mirror attached to the black lacquer triple dresser, she noticed a slight bulge in her abdomen. Ugh. With everything that had been going on between her and John, she hadn't found much time to exercise. Actually, no time. But this abdomen thing wasn't going to work. Especially since it had taken her six long months to get back into her twelves. That is, without being squeezed to death. And there was no way she was going to commence lugging around each and every one of those extra ten pounds she'd so miraculously been able to get rid of. She couldn't bear the thought of hearing those comments from her sickening relatives and so-called friends all over again. "Looks like you've put on a few pounds." "You look so different since you gained weight." And the worst one of all was the one that came from that big-mouth woman from church that day she'd seen her at the grocery store. "Karen? Is that you? I almost didn't recognize you since you've put on so much weight." A strange statement coming from a heifer whose butt was wide, high, and slouchy enough to sit an entire set of luggage on it.

The longer Karen gazed at her body in the mirror, the more disgusted she became. There was no question. She was going to have to start back getting on that treadmill every morning before going to work and meeting Regina at the health club on Saturday mornings.

Other than weight, Karen really didn't have any other physical characteristics to complain about. God had blessed her with a smooth, unblemished, medium chocolate complexion, and her hair was shoulder length and jet-black in color. Although she usually wore it back in a ponytail, thinking it was too coarse, not realizing that most black women would kill to acquire hair of that length and texture, and the ones who weren't willing to go to that extreme merely went to one of those Asian beauty supply houses and bought them some.

BEHIND CLOSED DOORS

When she reached her arms up to tighten the black silk scarf wrapped around her head, she took special notice of the edges around her hairline. She had thought she could go two more weeks without getting a touch-up, but shoot, these naps right here were saying no later than next Friday. She'd have to call Luanne first thing tomorrow morning to make sure she could get an appointment sometime before the end of next week.

She walked over to the window and once again looked through the mini-blind. *The least he could have done was call to let me know where he's at.* But John wasn't crazy. Last week when he'd decided to phone Karen from the track, she'd called him everything but a child of God. Even used the F word, something that had never parted her lips until he'd started messing up their money. Now, though, that horrible word seemed to roll right off her tongue with ease. And there had been major changes with other words in her vocabulary as well. She'd always used petty cuss words from time to time like anybody else did, but now *shoot* had mostly become *shit*, *butt* had seriously become *ass*, and *darn* was straight up *damn*.

By now, Karen's head was starting to pound, so she walked back over to the bed, lay down, and shut her eyes. Without even checking her blood pressure, she knew it was sky high. When she had gone for her yearly exam last week, the doctor had informed her that her blood pressure was one hundred fifty over ninety-five, and Karen knew she had to take this seriously, since her mother had been recently diagnosed with high blood pressure and her grandmother had struggled with it until the day she passed away three years ago. Not to mention the fact that it was one of the most common health problems among African-Americans today.

When she'd gotten her blood pressure checked during wellness week at the bank, the nurse had informed her that it was borderline high, and that she should consult her physician immediately. That was four weeks ago, and since it didn't seem to be stabilizing, her doctor had written her a prescription for a medication called Dyazide and suggested that she purchase a blood pressure monitor so she could take readings on a regular basis. Before Karen had left the clinic, the female physician had asked her if she was going through any unusual stress, but Karen had told her no. She wasn't sure why she had lied, though, because it clearly didn't take a rocket scientist to figure out that she had been under an excessive amount of stress—for the last two months, to be exact. Here she was reluctantly making withdrawals from their savings account, trying terribly to make ends meet, and arguing with John every single Friday about the problem he swore he didn't have. It was a wonder she hadn't had a stroke.

Karen couldn't understand how after five years of a near-perfect marriage, John could pick up this crazy obsession with gambling. He'd always played two or three dollars every day in the lottery and sometimes five or ten on the weekend, but not once had he ever mentioned going to the horse track. She wasn't sure what she was going to do if he didn't stop these weekly rendezvous, because John was the kind of husband most women only dreamed about, and the thought of losing or having to get rid of him gave her an eerie and uneasy feeling.

With twenty years at Chrysler's auto assembly plant, he was definitely secure in his job as a tool and die maker, and until now, he'd always brought his money home. Plus, the man spent all of his time with her, the one thing she and Regina loved about their husbands the most. It was so ironic how they had both been able to find that one particular quality in the men they chose to marry. Of course, anything was possible, and no one should ever say never, but deep down inside, she'd always felt that John would be faithful to her until the very end. Not because she thought she was God's gift to the world but because this man had proven his faithfulness to her for five years; unlike when she was married before, she never had to worry about what he might be doing out in the streets or, more importantly, who he might be out there doing it with. There was no doubt about it. This man loved her more than anything, and the feeling she had for him was the same.

Regina was always carrying on and on about how good a man John was, and Karen's mother loved John like her own son, as if she'd actually given birth to him. This, of course, was just the opposite of Karen's relationship with John's mother. That woman gave the word *mother-in-law* a new definition: bossy, two-faced, nosy, controlling, hypocritical, conniving, sneaky, and just plain sickening. Hell. She was honey, but even the bees didn't want anything to do with her. It was amazing how a woman like that could actually produce a child that had turned out to be as warm and loving as John. But then, of course, miracles do happen.

This woman despised all three of her daughters-in-law, mainly because they had married her precious little boys—little boys who were now in their late thirties. But Karen and her sisters-in-law couldn't care less if she liked them or not, because they'd long stopped caring about the ground she walked on anyway. The woman had disliked Karen since the first day they'd met and had downright begged John not to marry her. "You don't know nothin' about that woman. Somethin' just not right about her. You can't trust her one bit. All she wants you for is your money." *Money?* Last Karen had checked, she'd been working and supporting herself long before she'd even known who a John Jackson was.

But it was always about money when it came to John's mother, because before her sons had wives, "Mommie Dearest" had been receiving financial handouts from all three of her offspring. Sometimes on a weekly basis. That, of course, had come to a screeching halt when each of them had entered holy matrimony, and "Mommie D" has never gotten over it.

She'd tried every trick in the book to stop her baby from marrying Karen, and tonight was the first time Karen wished her mother-in-law had succeeded. At least then she wouldn't be sitting her butt here like some helpless child, waiting for his broke ass to get home.

Just as she opened her eyes and turned to look at the clock again, she heard the garage door opening. It was twelve-thirty. She sprang up from the bed, took large steps over to the window, looked down toward the driveway, and shook her head in amazement. She saw John sitting in their black Beamer waiting to pull into the garage. She couldn't believe he was still driving it to work. The transmission had started acting up during the middle of last week, and she had pleaded with him not to drive it until he could get it in and have it repaired. Damn. Why did he always have to be so hardheaded? All he was going to do was make bad matters worse. This man's head was equivalent to steel. Come to think of it, the note on the Beamer was due next Wednesday, and she was willing to bet he didn't have one nickel to pay it. They could pick the shit up for all she cared, because she wasn't withdrawing one red cent to pay for a car she hardly drove in the first place.

By now, she felt a sticky moisture pouring down from her underarms. She was angrier than she thought. It felt like it was one hundred degrees, but she knew that was far from possible for Schaumburg, Illinois. As a matter of fact, during the month of April, those living in the Chicago area were lucky if the temperature even hit seventy.

Karen hurried out of the master bedroom, into the hallway, and down the open staircase. Today she wished they had bought that ranch-style house down the street instead of this two-story, because by the time she'd stepped on the bottom stair, the alarm system was already going off and John was inside. She had wanted to be at the back door right when he opened it, but getting down the stairs had caused her a short delay.

She proceeded through the great room with a highly accelerated walk and then charged into the dining room. When she snapped on the light, John was standing at the other end of the glass dining room table and reaching toward the 15-button, ADT keypad, and from the astonished look on his face, she could tell he hadn't expected to see her standing there.

For a split second, she'd forgotten how upset she was, because the man was looking as gorgeous as ever. Like her, he had jet-black hair, a smooth, chocolate complexion, and he was tall. Six one, to be exact. His black Guess jeans, complimented by a black Guess sweatshirt, were perfectly starched, and he looked as though he should have been in this month's—no, every—issue of GQ magazine.

But so much for good looks. "Where the hell have you been?" she screamed.

At first there was silence, but from the look on his wife's face, John knew he had better respond with something. Even if it was a lie. "I drove into Rockford to visit my mother, and then met a couple of the guys from work for a drink."

"You know damn well you're telling a got-damn lie.

You've had your ass at the horse track all night, and now you're trying to pretend you've been somewhere else? Hell, you must think I'm stupid or something."

"I did stop by—"

Karen stepped closer to John and cut his explanation off. "Stop the bullshit, John. All I want to know is how much fuckin' money you lost this time?" She couldn't believe it. She'd just used that F word again. This was definitely going too far. This man was making her lose all of her religion, and it was going to have to cease. Her grandmother was probably doing a three-sixty turn in her grave by now, and her mother would go straight into cardiac arrest if she ever heard a word like that slipping out of her daughter's mouth. "One hundred, two hundred, three hundred, four hundred?"

John just stared at her and kept shifting his weight from one foot to the other. How was he going to tell her he'd lost his entire paycheck? He was better off dead.

"How much?"

"All of it." He couldn't believe he'd just said that shit. While driving home, he had decided to tell Karen that he'd only lost one hundred dollars. He was planning to borrow the other seven hundred and some odd dollars from his brother, Derrick, tomorrow. Derrick had helped him out when he'd lost his entire paycheck three weeks ago, but fortunately for him, Karen was unaware of it.

"Over eight hundred dollars? I just knew it. I hope you realize I'm not going to keep putting up with this shit? How in the hell do you plan on paying the note on that

BMW next Wednesday? Did you think about that? How in the hell do you think we're going to make ends meet if you keep taking your irresponsible ass to the track every Friday? I'm sick of this shit, and to tell you the truth, I'm sick of you. You need to grow up. I don't know what your problem is, but you'd better fix it or you're getting the hell out of here. I can do bad by myself, so I sure as hell don't need some gambling addict like you helping me. This shit is so typical. As soon as two black people start building something good together, one of them always tries to find a way to tear it down. Hell, if I wanted a man who throws his money away, I could've stayed married to that jackass I divorced six years ago."

John looked at Karen as if he didn't know who she was. He could clearly see that it was his wife standing in front of him, but it was the tone of her voice and choice of words that confused him. She was starting to make a habit of this. Lately, it had been hard to believe that this was the same woman who had graduated from high school in three years in a college preparatory program, maintained a 3.8 grade point average while completing her bachelor's degree in finance at the University of Illinois in Champaign, and completed an MBA program with honors while working full-time. And it definitely didn't sound like the same woman who was usually offended when he or anyone else used an excessive amount of vulgarity while in her presence. Shit, she was reminding him of those women he had seen on one of the talk shows a couple of weeks ago, when he'd skipped work and gone to the track. He couldn't remember if it had been Oprah, Sally, or Jenny he was watching, but that really didn't matter. What did matter was that those women were being verbally abused by their husbands, and he felt like he was getting the same treatment from Karen.

"Don't you have anything to say?" Karen asked.

"What do you want me to say? I mean, I'm sorry for what I did, but I know you don't want to hear—"

"You're damn right, I don't want to hear that shit."

If she was going to keep cutting him off, why did she ask him if he had anything to say? "I don't know what else to say, except I'm sorry and that I really learned my lesson tonight. This was the last time I'll be going out to Arlington on a Friday evening. Or any evening for that matter. So help me God."

"I think you better leave God out of this. Especially since you know you're not telling the truth. You don't even know what the truth is when it comes to gambling. You need to check the yellow pages for some help, because you obviously can't stop this crap on your own."

"I don't need any help. I've got this all under control. Tonight was the last night. You can believe that."

"I'm not believing shit, because you've been giving me that same sob story for the last three weeks, and I'm not listening to it anymore. Either you're going to cut it out or get the hell out of this house. Take your pick, brother."

Karen flipped the light switch to the off position as hard as she could and stormed through the great room, leaving John standing there in the dark. She couldn't see too well, and without paying much attention, she jammed her baby toe on the edge of the antique-white pillar at the base of the stairway. She screamed and then instantly reached down for her toe, grasping it as tight as she could. The pain raced through her entire foot. This was the same toe she had struck on the corner of the bed last Friday when she had been, once again, arguing with John, and she hoped like hell she hadn't broken it this time. Damn, he was already causing her major heartaches and mental distress, but now this shit was starting to get physical.

After she hopped back up to the second level, she opened the linen closet and pulled out a royal blue comforter and a pillow, went back over to the top of the stairs, and threw them both down to the main floor. "You can sleep on the basement sofa, the floor, or wherever, just so long as you don't bring your trifling ass up here."

John was standing at the bottom of the stairs about to take his first step up when the comforter struck him in the face. "You can't be serious. Do you actually think I'm going to sleep on the floor or the sofa, when we've got a huge guest bedroom upstairs? Woman, you must be crazy."

Karen scrunched her face. "Maybe you didn't hear me. I said, I don't want your ass up here. I don't want you anywhere near me." She walked into the master bedroom and slammed the door so hard that she turned and looked back at it to make sure the wood hadn't cracked.

She dove facedown across the bed, crying silently yet uncontrollably. She wasn't sure if she was sobbing because they were having their first major marital problem and it was getting out of hand, or if it was solely because he was messing up their money. Either way, she had to make him see that she was serious. That she wasn't just playing games with him. If he believed she would actually throw him out—which she didn't know if she could—just maybe he'd stop acting like some stark-raving, wild madman and get back to being the perfect husband he used to be.

CHAPTER 3

WHEN REGINA PULLED UP in her black Jeep Cherokee, she saw Karen stepping out of her white one. Their college dreams of getting married, owning two beautiful homes in an upper-class, Northwest suburb of Chicago, and having annual household incomes over one hundred thousand dollars had come true. Since the age of six they'd done just about everything together and purchased almost everything alike—mostly because Regina literally couldn't sleep at night if Karen had gone out and bought something and she, for whatever reason, hadn't yet been able to acquire it herself. Like last year, when the LeBaron convertible had been paid off. Karen had decided that she wanted a white, sun-roofed, gold-packaged Jeep Cherokee for the weekends, and when John had discovered they could purchase it at a price discounted by four thousand dollars, courtesy of his employee discount, they'd gone for it. Larry, on the other hand, thought thirty thousand was a ridiculous amount of money to pay for any vehicle that wasn't foreign made, he being a Lexus man and all, but Regina wasn't hearing any of that. All she'd wanted to know when she and Larry had arrived at the car dealership was how quickly they could prepare the paperwork in order for her to drive the Jeep off the lot the same day. Especially since Karen had already been driving hers for two weeks. Larry had kept reminding her that the only reason she wanted a Jeep was that Karen had one, although Regina would have rather died before admitting it.

"Why do you always have to keep up with everything John and Karen do. If Karen hadn't wanted a Cherokee, the thought of buying one would have never even entered your mind, and you know it."

But Regina insisted she had always had her heart set on buying one way before she'd even heard Karen mention anything about it. But Larry had known she was lying. And that was because she was.

Regina locked her doors with the black, keyless entry gadget hanging from her key ring, set the digital alarm system, and traveled across two aisles of the freshly blacktopped parking lot to where Karen was standing.

"Girl, you know if you hadn't called me this morning, I was definitely calling you," Regina said, smiling. "You've been missing these classes left and right."

"Yeah, I know, but under the circumstances I haven't had a mind to do anything. Not anything at all."

Regina didn't like the expression she saw on Karen's face or the sadness in her voice. "What's the matter, girl? You know I can always tell when something's wrong."

Karen tilted her head to the side as if to say *Guess,* and Regina knew immediately that John must have been out gambling again.

"What's up with that? Have you tried to talk him into getting help or going to Gamblers Anonymous? I've heard that those support groups can really make a difference when someone has an addiction problem."

Karen leaned against the Jeep and rested her backside on it. "Girl, I've tried everything, and all he does is say he's not going to the horse track when he gets paid next week, but then needless to say, when next week comes, he ends up there anyway. I gave him a nice cussing out and a serious ultimatum last night, though, so I'm sure he'll think twice before going to Arlington this coming Friday."

"I sure hope so, because you know this can't keep going on if you want to live the same lifestyle you're living now. That is, in a comfortable fashion."

Karen resented that last comment, because Regina was always spending over her budget for unnecessary items and then complaining about how difficult it was to make ends meet. As a matter of fact, she was starting to spend a nice chunk of money on those three- and four-digit lottery tickets herself. So, what did she know about being financially comfortable? Obviously, not one thing. Karen decided to ignore what Regina had said, though, because if she didn't, she might end up saying something she'd regret. It was better to just change the subject. "Where did you and Larry go last night?"

Regina glanced over in another direction, not wanting to let on that Larry had gone out without her again. She didn't want Karen or anyone else to know that she suspected him of tipping out on her. At least not yet, but she went ahead and spilled her guts anyway. "Nothing really. Larry went with Ted to play cards, and I sat around microwaving some leftover Chinese food. That was about it."

"Whoa. Larry went out without you on a Friday night again? That's the third time, isn't it? And even worse, I can't believe you let him out," Karen joked.

"Shut up, Karen. It was only a card game, and nothing to worry about," Regina said and laughed, but she felt unsure of herself because, actually, she was worried. She wasn't about to offer that small piece of information, though, because as usual, she didn't want to reveal that she and Larry were starting to have problems. She wanted Karen to think they still had the perfect marriage. Regina and Karen were best friends, but something internally always seemed to make her feel like she was in some sort of competition with Karen. She didn't know why and she could never put her finger on it, but that's just the way it was—the way it had always been since they were small children growing up back at home.

Karen looked at her sports watch and noticed that it was eight forty-five. They only had fifteen minutes before the start of class. "We had better get inside so we can get a spot somewhere in front. You know how I hate it when we get stuck in the back of the room."

They walked through the tinted glass doors of Golf Road's Health Club, up the stairs, into the aerobics room and then took a seat on the lightly waxed wooden floor in the front row as planned. Luther Vandross's "Here and Now" from his *Songs* CD was playing. Karen started singing right along with him. She'd sworn that whenever she and John renewed their wedding vows, she was having someone sing that song while she walked down the church aisle.

"Girl, you know I love my Luther. The man can't be touched, shit, not even slightly tapped when it comes to singing love songs," Karen said.

They both laughed. "Girl, if Luther knew how much you loved his music, he'd probably fly in here and sing the song for you himself."

Karen sang and swayed her head from side to side with her eyes closed, not paying much attention to what Regina had just said.

Regina smiled, then looked toward the entryway. "I wonder where Marilyn is."

"Please. She'll be here. You know Miss Thing never misses."

"You are so crazy," Regina said. "You're just jealous because she works out so religiously and would still have a body like Halle Berry even if she didn't."

"You're right, and it's sickening too."

They both laughed.

Actually, Karen had never cared for Marilyn because she'd always believed Marilyn was jealous of Regina. Always finding something to criticize her about: "You look like you've picked up a few pounds, girlfriend." "It's about time to get that hair cut, isn't it?" "What do you guys need with a Mercedes, Lexus and a Jeep? All you have is a two-car garage." Just the thought of Marilyn and her remarks made Karen cringe. She couldn't stand the wench.

Regina turned toward the door again and said, "Speaking of the devil." Marilyn walked in, and Regina motioned for her to come and sit with them. As if she'd sit anywhere else. For one, she and Regina were good friends and had been ever since they'd all enrolled at U of I twelve years ago. Secondly, there weren't very many African-American women living in Schaumburg, and the ones who did reside there never seemed to frequent this particular health club anyway. Not long ago, Karen had tried to persuade one of the sisters at the bank to become a member, but she'd said that she already had a membership at the one in Elgin. For a split second, Karen had wondered why the sister would rather drive twenty minutes or more to Elgin when there was a club right here in the suburb where she lived, but when it dawned on her how many blacks lived out there, the reason was evident.

Marilyn dropped down on the rubber mat next to Regina. "Hey, Gina. Hey, Karen."

"Hey, girl," Regina said and crossed her legs.

"How's it going?" Karen asked, trying to be cordial.

"With the exception of me running a little late, I'm fine."

"We still have about ten minutes before the instructor starts the warm-up music, so you really haven't missed anything," Regina said.

Marilyn reached down to tie her Reeboks and then looked over at Regina's. "It's about time for some new Rees, don't you think?"

That bitch. Karen wanted to knock Marilyn's ass across that floor they were sitting on, but since that wasn't her style, she decided against it. Hmmph.

"Girl, please," Regina said, trying wholeheartedly to play the whole thing off. "These shoes are expensive, and I'm getting as much wear and tear out of them as I can."

Marilyn looked at Regina with a catty expression and was preparing to make another snide remark when she glanced over and saw Karen staring at her like a dog anxiously awaiting his prey.

Regina noticed the same thing and hurried to change the subject. "So what's up with the love life these days?" she asked Marilyn.

"Shit, I'm sick of men, period. Whenever the sex is great, the man is no earthly good, but when the man is sweet, considerate and successful, his dick is no bigger than a Popsicle stick. Either way, you can't win."

"You're sick, girl," Regina said and laughed.

Karen was still pissed off about that Reebok remark, but she couldn't resist the urge to crack up at what Miss

Thing had just said, because those had been her thoughts exactly before she'd met John. During college, she'd dated this Wesley Snipes-looking guy named James and had gone out with him for a whole two months before even entertaining the idea of having sex with him. Then, one night after a sorority party and a few too many wine coolers, she'd let her hair down. Practically dragged him to her apartment—something she couldn't have done if she and Regina had still been living in that all-girls dorm.

Karen had slipped off her dress and laid across the bed, while James had removed his jeans and sweatshirt. So far so good. Then brotherman pulled down his briefs. And that's when the bombshell went off. She couldn't believe it. Such a big personality, with all of two or three inches between his legs. She'd felt sorry for the poor man, but there was no way on earth he was depositing that little thing inside of her. Shoot, even banks had a minimum balance requirement for opening an account, and her guidelines were exactly the same.

"Don't worry, Marilyn, you will find Mr. Right, get married, and live happily ever after," Regina said.

"Married? Don't count on it. As far as I'm concerned, all men are dogs and married ones are nothing more than dogs on a leash."

Marilyn and Karen chuckled, but Regina didn't see anything too funny, since she was afraid that Larry was starting to slip into that same category.

"I can't believe you haven't met a lot of brothers through work," Regina said. "I mean, you've been working for that training firm for over two years now, and you're down in the Loop all the time working with so many different companies."

"I don't know. You tell me what's up," Marilyn said. "Maybe I don't look good enough for the brothers around here. Shit, something must be wrong."

"Marilyn, please." Regina didn't know what Marilyn could possibly be talking about. She had everything going for her in the looks department. She was tall, and even though she was dark-skinned, she was beautiful. As a matter of fact, she and Karen were the two most beautiful dark-skinned sisters Regina knew. Not to mention the fact that all of Marilyn's curves were in their right places. If there was a reason behind her not being able to find the right man, one thing was for sure, her looks had nothing to do with it.

Regina glanced up and saw Tina, their aerobics instructor, walking to the front. "We'd better stand up. I think Tina's ready to start."

Karen watched Tina take out the Luther CD, pop in one by Toni Braxton, and press the Program button on the CD player. "Love Should Have Brought You Home Last Night" started playing, which was too slow for an aerobic workout, but more than sufficient for their initial stretching exercises. This CD was every bit of three years old, but this white girl knew she had excellent taste when it came to R & B music. Never played anything else.

Probably had something to do with that brother she'd been dating for the last two years.

R EGINA WAS A million miles away, but she felt as though Toni was singing directly to her. Last night, Larry had phoned her from the car phone saying he and Ted were stopping at Studebakers for a quick drink, but then he hadn't shown his face at home until after two-thirty. When he'd called, it had been eleven-thirty. It surely didn't take three hours to have a quick drink, drop Ted off, and get his butt home. Studebakers, Ted's bachelor pad, and Wesleyan Estates were all within a three- to four-mile radius of each other. He must have thought she was Boo Boo the Fool or something. She'd confronted him as soon as he'd taken off his clothes and gotten into bed, but all he'd kept saying was how he didn't know where the time had gone, and he'd even seemed a little perturbed at the fact that she was questioning him about it.

"Look, Regina. I'm tired, and I don't feel like going through this shit all over again. I just told you not more than two seconds ago that I lost track of time. What else do you want me to say?"

"How could you lose track of time for three whole hours?" she had asked him. "Something's not right with this, and I want to know what's really going on here."

"You're just paranoid. You've been paranoid and un-sure of yourself ever since the day I met you, and I'm sick of you taking it out on me. There's nothing going on, and you know it."

"No, I don't know anything. But what I do know is that you're starting to go out without me on a regular basis, and whenever a man starts doing that, something is usually going on."

"Look, damn it. I know where this is headed, and I'm telling you, I don't want to hear it. I'm sick of all this nagging. Why don't you turn over and go to sleep," Larry had said, raising his voice.

"I don't want to go to sleep, and I don't appreciate you talking to me like that and telling me what I should or shouldn't do. I'll go to sleep when I damn well please."

"Well, talk to yourself then, because I'm not saying another word. Not tonight or any night. I'm not some child that needs to check in or explain what I'm doing every time I leave the house."

Larry had turned his back to her and was snoring no sooner than he'd spoken the last word of his sentence. Regina could still picture herself lying there with tears rolling down the sides of her face and onto the pillow. This man had gone out, enjoyed the company of God knows who, and, unlike her, was getting a good night's sleep. He didn't seem to care about her feelings at all anymore. There was something very wrong with him. Something wrong with them. She couldn't help but fear what that mysterious something was.

CHAPTER 4

I NSTEAD OF MISSING ONLY a few sessions, Karen's body felt like she hadn't worked out in months. She was dog tired and convinced that every muscle in her body would be sore by evening. Lying across her good comforter was forbidden, but today she didn't care. She'd always fussed at John about coming home from work and plopping down on their perfectly made-up bed, but right now, she understood precisely why he did. It felt good. She couldn't dare let him see her enjoying it, though, because he would somehow mistakenly assume that the comforter was open game and that the rules had changed. That he could spread out on it whenever he was ready.

Karen heard John coming up the staircase. She sprang up off the bed, carefully smoothed the comforter with both hands, and moved toward the closet, pretending to gather together dirty clothes that needed dry cleaning. Although not much pretending was necessary, since she had seven suits, five silk blouses, and three dresses that terribly needed to be dropped off at Big Bear Laundry.

John walked up behind her, wrapped both of his arms around her, and kissed her passionately on her neck. Chills ran through her entire body, and all she was capable of was closing her eyes and enjoying it. He knew what that did to her, and she wished he would stop it. How could she continue being angry with him when he was making her feel so good? She wanted to fight him. But not really. She was helpless and loved it.

"I love you more than anything in this world," John said. "I would never do anything to lose you, and I'm so sorry for what I've been doing. I know I've been screwing up our money, but I promise I won't ever do that again."

Why was he bringing this up now? She had just decided they would argue after they made love. He was breaking the mood and sounding no different than he had last week when he'd given her this same tired story. She really wanted to believe him, but she had to make him see that she wasn't going to continue putting up with this kind of behavior. Had to let him know that she meant business.

She lifted both of his hands from her body and spun around to face him. He had that innocent, little-boy expression, and she almost felt sorry for him. But this was not the time for sympathy.

"John, you've been promising me every week that

you'll come straight home from work on Friday and not go to the track, but so far, you haven't kept your word one time. We can't go on like this. I've done all the withdrawing, transferring, rearranging, and tolerating I can stand, and like I told you last night, I can do bad by myself. You have a commitment to me and this marriage, and you're not holding up your end of the deal. We have a lot of love between us, and it doesn't make sense to throw it all away simply because you refuse to own up to the problem you know you have. Why won't you just admit that you need help?"

"I told you I've got this under control. I'm not some crazy person who needs to converse with a group of troubled individuals who don't know whether they're going or coming."

"People who go to Gamblers Anonymous aren't crazy. If anything, they're intelligent. Because unlike a lot of people, they've put aside their petty pride and gotten their acts together."

"I'll tell you what, if I don't bring my paycheck home this Friday, then I'll go to Gamblers Anonymous. No ifs, ands, or buts about it."

"If you don't bring your paycheck home this Friday, you won't have to worry about it at all, because you won't be living here. And I mean that."

John laughed, but Karen didn't see anything amusing.

"I'm telling you, baby, I'm not going to gamble anymore. I mean, I might spend a couple dollars here and there with the lottery, but that's about it. I promise."

He was making way too many promises for one conversation, and Karen was skeptical. She hoped he was going to do what he said, though, because if he didn't, there was going to be serious trouble in paradise one week from now.

"We'll see what happens, but I still say you should go to one of those meetings this week. Better yet, sometime today. I'll even go with you, if that's what it'll take to get you there."

"Everything will be fine. Don't worry about it."

"I can't help but worry. If I didn't, what would happen to the note on that BMW and all the rest of our bills that are due this week? I'll tell you what—they wouldn't get paid. But by me worrying, fussing and making damn sure that we have a decent savings account, it's not a problem."

"You're right, baby, and you know I appreciate the way you handle our finances. You know I've always been proud to have a wife with such a good head for money, and I love you for it."

It was true. John did love the way she handled their finances, and he was the first one to admit that he had horrible spending habits. But two months ago, Karen's handling of the finances had caused all hell to break loose. It was the day Chrysler had issued those enormous profit-sharing checks to its employees, and "Mommie D" had been sure she was going to get a piece of it. How wrong she'd been, though. Karen still couldn't believe what that woman had said about her. "John, it's a shame you don't have control over your own money. You've got that thing sittin' up over there collecting everythang." What a joke.

John moved toward Karen again. He placed both his muscular arms around her, squeezed tight, and kissed her like it was his last opportunity.

This time, she kissed him back. It hurt like hell when they argued, but making up always seemed to lessen the pain.

But last night had reminded her of how it had been with her first husband, who was nothing more than an irresponsible little boy, resting inside a grown man's body. He clearly wanted nothing to do with the idea of growing up. That man had been the husband from hell, and she'd never met anyone like him. He'd screwed around with any and every woman that would have him and told more lies in one day than Pinocchio could have conjured up in an entire year. And could look you straight in the face when he did it, too. She'd promised herself that if she ever came across another man that so much as resembled her ex-husband, she'd break and run from him like her life depended on it, making sure not to ever look back.

They slowly made their way to the bed and stretched across it with no time for turning back the comforter. John slid off Karen's workout pants, pulled her sleeveless leotard down her body, and removed her underwire bra and silk panties. He still had on a pair of silk briefs, but within seconds, his body was completely exposed.

He looked exceptionally fine, almost delicious, and Karen couldn't help but stare at him. He lunged on top of her, kissed her forehead, and gradually made his way down to all ten of her perfectly manicured toes. She didn't move. He kissed his way back toward her calves and then to her knees, but when he arrived at the spot located just below her abdomen, the rest was history.

Karen smiled softly and thought, "This man has it going on, and I'm not about to lose him. Not to gambling. Or anything else."

As soon as Regina noticed that Larry wasn't home, she got nervous. She'd only been at the health club for two hours, and here he was already gone. Hadn't left a note on the refrigerator or a personal memo on the answering machine. The man was taking these disappearing stints to the extreme, and something was going to have to be done about it.

Prior to the last few weeks, he would have never left the house without making sure she knew where he was. Where could he be at ten-thirty in the morning, anyway? This was getting to be too much for her to stomach. He wasn't giving her one ounce of respect. Maybe she shouldn't have given him the third degree last night, but she was his wife and had a right to know where he'd been. Everything was all wrong, and this situation was getting worse instead of better.

She started down the basement stairs, but heard the

phone ringing. Maybe it was Larry. She rushed back up the stairs, skipping most of them, and answered it. "Hello?"

"So, you're back."

He was sounding awfully chipper, and she wished she could smack the mess out of him. "As a matter of fact, I came straight home thinking you'd be here."

"Look. Before you get upset, let me explain. Ted wanted me to ride out to Oakbrook. Fields is having a men's suit sale, and you know I've been planning to get a couple for work."

Oh, Lord. She hoped Ted was picking them out for him, otherwise there was no telling what he might bring back with him. She pulled over a kitchen chair and sat down. "If he wanted you to ride with him, why isn't the Lexus in the garage?"

"Regina, please. You know I usually drive wherever I go. No matter who it's with. Why are you tripping?"

He sounded irritated. Something that was becoming routine. "I'm not tripping. I thought *we* were going to spend time together today, not you and Ted."

"We're in McDonald's drive-thru right now and should be at the mall in about thirty minutes. I should be home around two, and we'll plan something then. Okay?"

"Whatever, Larry."

"I wish you would stop being so paranoid. Nobody loves you more than I do, and you know it."

If he loved her so much, why was he all of a sudden

treating her this way? But right now, it wasn't even worth going into. "I'll see you when you get home."

"Bye, baby."

She reached the phone up and placed it on the hook, covered her face with both palms, and tried to figure this all out. Nothing was adding up. If it was another woman, he'd be gone a lot more than this. Wouldn't he? If he wasn't in love with her any longer, wouldn't he just ask for a divorce? But then, maybe he wanted to have his cake and eat it too, like most men.

This was like being on a roller coaster. No matter how she weighed it, there wasn't reason enough for Larry to be showing out the way he was. She needed desperately to confide in someone about this whole predicament. She wanted to call Karen, but since she might be jumping the gun, she pushed that idea completely out of her mind. There was still a chance Larry would come to his senses and go back to treating her like his wife. If he did, she wouldn't have to squeal this information to anyone.

She stood up from the table and started back down to the lower level. She hadn't done the wash in over two weeks, and with the two of them each using a fresh towel every day, they were almost completely out. Before long, they'd be tapping into their guest supply, and that never made any sense to her.

She set the wash cycle on the large-capacity Kenmore, pulled the knob to start it, and threw the towels in two and three at a time. Larry's racquetball clothes and her aerobic outfits were piled high and were going to be the next load. She sorted through Larry's shirts first, then his shorts. But when she went to pull out the pocket of his burgundy pair, she noticed a small yellow sticky note. When she unfolded it, she saw a phone number and a name written in blue ink. She was so taken aback by what she saw that her knees became weak, a heaviness twirled through her head, and eventually she had no choice but to grab hold of the washer for a few minutes.

The name was spelled R-O-N-I. There was no doubt. This was a female. Probably short for Veronica. "That's who he's been taking his no-good ass out of here to be with. He must think I'm stupid. I'll bet he's got his yellow ass at her house right now." Nobody was listening, but she didn't give a damn.

She walked into the rec room, over to the phone sitting on the wet bar, took the receiver off the hook, and dialed the number on the yellow piece of paper. It rang ten times, but there was no answer. She slammed the phone back on the hook. This whore wasn't even classy enough to have an answering machine or the voice mail feature offered through the local telephone company. She was probably home though, just too busy screwing Larry to answer any phone calls. Regina wanted to hurt both of them. She felt like killing Larry.

Regina was so upset that she could hear the pounding of her heartbeat, which was racing a thousand miles a minute. This was uncalled for. She had given this man two of the best years of her life. Loving him. Waiting on him hand and foot like her middle name was Kizzy.

Cooking his meals. Washing his filthy clothes. Having sex with him only a few times a week when she really wanted it every day. Her world more or less revolved around his, and this was the thanks she got? And all those nights she'd waited for him to get home from Trans-State Insurance when he'd claimed he was working overtime. His ass was working overtime all right. Literally. But Larry Moore wasn't getting away with this shit, though. Not as long as there was still air for her to breathe.

A FTER USELESSLY STEWING over the situation, Regina decided to go throw the towels in the dryer. She'd completely forgotten about them. Until now, she didn't think it was humanly possible to be pissed off, hurt, and scared all at the same time, but that's exactly what she was feeling now. She couldn't wait for Larry to bring his deceitful ass home so she could get to the bottom of this once and for all.

When she climbed back up the stairs, the phone rang. She wasn't in the mood for any phone calls, but she figured it might be Larry. If it was, she wasn't waiting until he got home. She was going off on him right now. "Hello?"

"Hey, Gina," her mother said.

"Hi, Ma. How are you?"

"I'm doing fine. How's Larry?"

She hated even answering that. If she told her mother

what her bastard-for-a-son-in-law was really doing, she'd be on the phone for the next couple of hours, and her mother would be worried sick. She worried about everything. This wasn't the time to upset her, especially since she was sounding so cheerful. "He's fine."

"When are you all coming to see us? It has been a while, you know."

"I know, Ma. We'll probably drive over there next Sunday. I'll talk to Larry and make sure we don't have any other plans." She wanted to say, make sure he didn't have any plans with his little whore.

"Good. Just let me know by next Friday, so I'll know how much to cook for dinner. I need plenty of time to plan out my menu and make groceries."

"You don't have to do that, Ma. We can take you out or something. You guys have all those new restaurants on East State Street, and I'll bet you two haven't been to more than one or two of them."

"Now Gina, you know I like to fix my Sunday dinners. And your father would have a fit if he and Larry couldn't sit around watching those Bulls bounce that silly ball around on television. I think that's the main reason he bought that forty-inch screen."

Regina laughed, because her mother was right. Her father wasn't the excitable type, but he always seemed thrilled when he knew Larry was coming for a visit. Not just to watch a game, but for any reason. As far as he was concerned, Larry was the son he and her mother were never able to have. After Regina was born, they had made one attempt after another trying to conceive a baby, but after the third miscarriage, they'd come to the realization that maybe it wasn't in God's plan for them to have more than one child. Regina figured that was why they'd always showered her with everything they could, from love to the most expensive clothing, to the brand-new white Escort they'd gotten her the very same day she'd turned sixteen.

Regina glanced outside the kitchen window and saw Larry pulling into the driveway. "Larry just got home, Ma, so I'll call you in a few hours, okay?"

"Girl, you better stay off that phone so much making all those long-distance phone calls. I'll just talk to you next Friday."

She didn't know why her mother was saying that. She knew Regina always called them at least four to five times a week, regardless of how much it cost. "I love you, Ma, and tell Daddy I said hi."

"I will. I love you too, baby. Bye."

Larry came in, slithered over to Regina like the snake that he was, put his forefinger under her chin, and kissed her. Regina shoved him away from her so hard that he stumbled against the kitchen table.

"What's the matter with you?" Larry asked, frowning, trying to steady his balance.

"What the hell do you think is the matter with me?" She picked up the sticky note from the table and pushed it into his chest. It stuck to his shirt.

Larry pulled it off, looked at it, and cracked up laughing. "What? You think this number is for me? You've got to be kidding."

"It was in your pocket. Who else is it for?"

"It's not for me. I got this number from Veronica Williams for Ted. She's a claims adjuster from work."

"If you got it from her at work, then why was it in your racquetball shorts? Huh? Explain that."

"I didn't say I got it from her at work. I mean, I had meant to, but I never got the chance to do it, because she works on a different floor. So when I saw her at the Mobile gas station last week, I got it from her then. But I keep forgetting to give it to Ted. As a matter of fact, he asked me about it last night."

"Now, Larry. Do you think I was just born yesterday?"

"No, but I'm telling you the truth. We can call Ted if you want to."

Regina didn't want that. Ted already thought she was paranoid and keeping track of Larry too much as it was. And, since Larry was explaining this so well and wanted to prove it, she sort of believed him.

"No. Just forget it. Ted doesn't have anything to do with this," Regina said.

"I think he has everything to do with this, because the phone number is for him." Larry reached for the phone.

She took it from his hand and put it back on the hook. "Okay. Okay. I believe you, but that still doesn't explain everything else you've been doing. Like all the lost time you've been accumulating."

"Not this again, Regina. Why can't we just enjoy the

day like you said you wanted to earlier? I realize I've been going out a little more than usual, but I promise you, I don't want anyone except you. Sometimes it's just good to get out with the fellas for a change. Why can't you please try and understand that?"

"But you've been canceling lunch every time we plan to go, and you've also been working an unusual amount of overtime. What about that?"

"What do you expect me to do? Let my work go undone? We've had a lot of insurance claims lately, and I'm still trying to hire two additional supervisors before the end of the month. What do you want me to do? Forget my priorities?"

Regina felt a lot better now than she had, because this was like the old Larry. Answering all of her questions and making some sense. She was stupid for suspecting him of messing around, and she was going to be more understanding the next time he went out. Even if it was next Friday on their movie night.

"I don't know what's wrong with me. I'm sorry for pushing you, and I'm sorry for accusing you of something you're not doing," Regina said, tears slowly flowing down her face.

Larry smiled and took her in his arms. "I'll let you slide this time, but it better not happen again."

His smile gave her a warm feeling inside, and she wished this moment would never end. He was holding her tighter than he had in a long time, and she was certain that they were about to make love like they never had before. The real Larry Moore was finally home again.

CHAPTER 5

KAREN STRUTTED into her newly decorated office located on the fifth floor of the bank, removed her purple linen blazer, hung it on the brass coat rack in the corner behind the door, and sat down behind her oak executive-style desk. She placed her black Coach purse in the lower right-hand drawer and set her matching briefcase on the floor. She could already tell that this was going to be a hectic workday and the beginning of another drawn-out, tiring week.

Ever since Bank First had gone through a difficult merger and extensive layoffs two months ago, which, incidentally, was around the same time John had become obsessed with going on those racing track excursions, Karen had taken on three times her normal job responsibilities. Attending meetings back to back. Supervising twice the number of employees. Laboring through just about every lunch hour. She couldn't remember when she had ever felt so stressed. It was a good thing Saturday and Sunday had turned out the way they had. She'd needed it.

Of course, Friday evening had started out on a terrible note, but the remainder of the weekend had been comprised of countless, uninterrupted episodes of lovemaking. That was how it had always been with her and John, and if she had anything to do with it, that was how it was going to stay. No children. No pets. And no nearby, do-drop-in relatives.

When they were first engaged, John had discussed having at least one child, but Karen had made it perfectly clear that children were not a part of her lifetime agenda. A decision made long before she'd even graduated from high school and the reason she'd had clips surgically clamped around each of her fallopian tubes. One of the more modern methods of sterilization. Her grandmother had insisted she would change her mind once she was older, found the right man, and fell deeply in love with him, but even though she was now less than two weeks from turning thirty and married to a man she couldn't love more, her feelings toward bringing a child into the world remained unchanged. It enraged her when different folks, mostly women who needed to mind their own business, asked her why she didn't want children. It was almost as if they thought she was crazy. Like it made her less than a woman. Like it meant the end of time. But she ignored them, because as far as she was concerned, it was better not to have children when you knew you didn't want them than to get pregnant because other people expected it and then regret it, like so many others she knew. She'd seen enough of that to last her a lifetime.

Oh, sure, she and John did have a good marriage, but that didn't seem to guarantee anything. Her own father had proven that thirteen years ago when he'd walked out on his faithful wife and two teenaged daughters, which was the main reason her younger sister, Sheila, the black sheep of the family, had turned out the way she had. He'd left without so much as saying good-bye, and until this day, he'd never contacted them. Sheila hadn't been able to deal with his leaving and had soon started interacting with the wrong element. Dating guy after guy, not one of whom had meant her any good, and hanging out with girls who'd looked forward to nothing except getting high and pumping out babies. Just thinking about Sheila and her many dilemmas depressed Karen, and since she had a pile of work to do, she decided that this wasn't the time to dwell on it.

She shuffled through two stacks of papers, searching for this month's loan activity report and found it. Whew. There hadn't been this many loan applications since the interest rates had been at an all-time low two years ago. Business was booming, and it was great for the bank. Not to mention the enormous bonus check she was sure to receive at the end of the quarter.

She flipped her calendar to the current date and released a deep sigh. Meetings were penciled in at eight, ten, one, and two-thirty. It was a good thing she'd decided to come in at seven. She hated going to meetings first thing on a Monday morning, and her secretary knew it, but then maybe it couldn't be helped. Nevertheless, Karen was going to present her secretary with another gracious reminder just in case.

She had thought her promotion from supervisor to vice president of Mortgage Loans would mean more leeway with decision making and fewer meetings to attend. But now, instead of simply attending the meetings, she'd taken on the responsibility of chairing them. It was a good thing they'd given her that ten-thousand-dollar raise, because if they hadn't, she'd have turned in her resignation a long time ago.

The sun was a tad too bright, so she swirled around in her plush, high-back chair and closed the blind halfway. As she turned back around, the phone rang. She removed her right pearl earring. "Good morning, this is Karen speaking."

"Hi, sweetie, how are you?"

"I'm fine, Mom. How are you?"

"I'm good. Are you busy?"

"No. Is everything okay?"

"Everything's fine. I got a little worried when I didn't hear from you all weekend and thought I'd give you a call."

"I know, Mom. I'm sorry I didn't get a chance to call you. Time just sort of slipped by me the last couple of days."

"You and John must have been honeymooning."

Karen laughed. "As a matter of fact, we were. We really had a good time this weekend. Better than we have in a long time."

"I'm glad, because I know how upset you've been since he started going to that horse track."

"Actually, he went out there again on Friday, but I gave him one last ultimatum. Mom, he spent his whole paycheck, and it would have been more than that if he didn't have ten percent coming out for his 401(K) plan."

"Lord have mercy. Well, maybe this is just a phase he's going through, because the John I know is too sensible to keep doing something like this forever."

"Phase or not, I told him that I'm not going to put up with it anymore, and if he did it one more time, he was getting out."

"Karen. Don't be so hard on him. Until now, John's been bringing home his entire paycheck and giving you every dime of it. Not a whole lot of men would do that. John is a good man, and if gambling is the only fault he has, you can work with him on that. I'm not saying his problem is something you can overlook, but nobody's perfect. And having a man who gambles is a lot better than having one who messes around with other women or one who tries to beat you half to death."

"I'm trying to keep an open mind, but I refuse to keep withdrawing money from our savings accounts because of this terrible habit he's picked up. Pretty soon, there won't be anything *to* withdraw."

"Maybe you can get him to go to one of those sup-

port group meetings. You know, one of those anony-
mous ones."

"I mentioned that to him, but all he says is that he
doesn't have a problem, and he's not going to the track
anymore. But he's said that every week since this all
began. I just hope things are different this Friday."

"They will be. You know John doesn't want to lose
you, so he'll think twice before doing it again. You just
have to trust in the Lord is all."

"I know, and I hope that's all it takes, because I don't
know what else to do. How is your shoulder doing?"

Slaving at an assembly plant as a drill operator for the last
thirty years had finally taken its toll. Karen's mother had
been diagnosed with a tear in her left rotator cuff and had
gone through surgery over two months ago, but the healing
process was taking a lot longer than usual—at least longer
than it had for the right shoulder when she'd had the same
procedure performed on it just a year ago. "It seems to be
doing a little better today. I have therapy this afternoon."

"When do you think you'll be going back to work?"

"I don't know. I went to the doctor on Thursday, and
he doesn't want to see me again for three weeks. Maybe
he'll release me then. Who knows."

Lucinda was sounding frustrated, and that troubled
Karen. "Has the company found a job that won't reinjure
your shoulders when you do go back to work?"

"Not one I know of. But they'd rather see me walking
around doing nothing than out on worker's compensa-
tion, causing their loss time report to skyrocket."

"What about your settlement? Have you heard anything from your attorney?"

"No, but we should be settling on the right shoulder sometime next month. It'll probably be a long time before they even begin negotiations for this left one, though."

"Well, at least you'll be getting compensated for some of what you've gone through."

"Not really. They can't pay me enough for all the suffering I've had to deal with and the pain that has kept me up all hours of the night, and I'll never have a full range of motion with either shoulder ever again."

"Yeah, I guess you're right about that."

"Well, I don't want to stay on this phone too long, and I know you have to get to work."

Karen had known that was coming, and she smiled.

"Yeah, I do. I've got meetings all day, but I'll give you a call tonight after dinner."

"Have a good day at work, and I'll talk to you then."

"Bye, Mom."

There were no words to describe the relationship between Karen and her mother. Lucinda was fifty-one and looked not a day over forty. Whether they strolled through a shopping mall or dined at a fancy restaurant, most everyone assumed they were sisters. Her mother was a beautiful woman. Kept her weight down, hair in place, makeup intact, and dressed immaculately at all times. But the physical aspects were only part of the package. Her personality shined, and she had a heart that reached out to everyone, regardless of who it was.

She'd become the second mother to every friend Karen had, something that had hardly been the case when Karen was between the ages of twelve and seventeen.

Practically every girl on the block had, at one time or another, harassed, ridiculed, or criticized Karen for having a warden for a mother. Most of them had never even heard of the word *curfew* and hadn't had one. Karen had always been the earliest thing leaving the neighborhood park, the local skating rink, and any Saturday night parties, which really hadn't mattered too much, since there had only been a few, rare occasions when she had actually been allowed to darken the doorway of any of those places anyhow. Back then, the woman had pretty much made Karen sick by keeping her locked up in prison. But now Karen clearly understood why her mother had, because those same neighborhood girls who'd had the freedom to roam any- and everywhere they'd wanted, all times of the night, were now high school dropouts, unmarried with a house full of babies they couldn't take care of, or out on the street begging some low-life drug dealer for a piece of that illegal white rock. All situations that Karen didn't envy one bit.

She gathered together a pad of legal-sized paper, an ink pen, a neon green highlighter, then glanced at her watch. There was still twenty minutes before the start of the weekly status meeting, and since she saw her voice mail light flashing at the base of her phone, she decided to retrieve whatever messages had been left. She pressed the speaker button first but then decided against it and lifted the receiver instead. Just three months ago, she'd played a message through her speaker phone only to hear John dictating exact details of what he was going to do to her that night when she arrived home. She'd been loving every bit of it until she'd noticed her secretary standing inside the doorway, with a cherry red face and no obvious sign of movement. The woman had been in a severe state of shock, and Karen had been speechless. What could she possibly have said? Nothing she could have thought of would have corrected it, so it had been better to leave it alone and let it blow over.

Karen keyed in her numerical password and waited for the messages. The first was from Tammy, her boss's secretary, saying it was that time of year again and she needed to schedule Karen's performance evaluation. The last one was from John, saying he was on his morning break and that he wanted a complete reenactment of what had gone on this past weekend. Tonight. Whipped cream, strawberries, Pink Champale, and all.

That did it. She was never using that speaker phone again. At least not with her door wide open, because John's messages were way too X rated, and the man was too nasty for his own good. Although, she couldn't help but admit, she loved it.

"DON'T FORGET to pick up some of that tropical sparkling water we always get at the store on Roselle," Karen yelled down the stairs to John, who was on his way out for pizza. Then she switched the radio station from WGCI to V103. She wasn't in the mood for any gangsta rap and wanted to listen to something a lot more mellow.

"I won't," John yelled back and then went out the door.

It was only after coming home, tearing their clothes off, and doing exactly what John had suggested on the voice mail message that they'd realized how starved they were. With the exception of the strawberries, neither of them had had a thing to eat since lunchtime. She'd left work at three-thirty so she could meet John at home by four, but now it was almost seven.

Karen was no remarkable cook, didn't care to become one, and had no problem with eating carry-out every night of the week. But John, on the other hand, despised consuming anything that wasn't home-cooked. That is, unless it came from Red Lobster, Bennigan's or Lone Star Steakhouse. As a matter of fact, today was the first time in a long time that he seemed content with the idea of ordering a pizza, and Karen wondered why he was so willing. But it was obvious. He was still in beg mode because of all the money he'd donated to Arlington's race track on Friday night. Right now she could probably get him to throw his dirty clothes in the hamper instead of smearing them across the bed in the guest bedroom. Shoot, she could probably even get him to wash dishes every night for the rest of the week and take the trash out without being told.

V103 wasn't playing anything she wanted to hear either, so she flipped the radio off and clicked on the television. It would take John at least twenty to thirty minutes to get back, and she figured she'd pass the time by calling her sister, Sheila. She picked up the latest issue of *Ebony,* then dialed the number. As she hit the last digit of the phone number, she realized Sheila might not be home yet, because today was check day, and whenever that welfare money came, the girl usually flew straight to Wal-Mart and stayed until closing. It had taken Rockford forever to get a Wal-Mart store, but ever since it had, Sheila had become one of their most frequent and loyal customers. There was no more Kmart for her. Girlfriend had moved up in the world.

"Hello," Sheila answered.

"Hey, Sheila. What are you doing at home?"

"I live here, don't I?" Sheila said and laughed.

"Keep getting smart, okay?"

"What are you and John up to?"

"Not much. John just went out to pick up a pizza, and I'm sitting here flipping through this month's *Ebony.*"

"Picking up a pizza? Not the John I know?"

Karen smiled. "I didn't believe it either at first, but he's going along with anything I want right now because I got so upset with him for losing his whole paycheck at the track. Didn't Mom tell you about it?"

"No, but I haven't talked to her today, either."

Somehow, that didn't surprise Karen. Sheila was living right there in the same town with their mother, but she hardly ever bothered to pick up the phone to see how

Lucinda was doing. Sheila had somehow gotten it in her head that if Lucinda had been a better wife, their father would have never deserted them—something that couldn't have been further from the truth.

"Why haven't you?" Karen asked.

"You know I get my check on the twenty-fourth, and I've been running around here and there all day."

Karen didn't say anything, so Sheila continued the conversation. "I'll bet you went off on him, didn't you?"

"You know I did. Things like that have to be nipped in the bud right away before they spin too far out of control."

"You probably told him he was getting out if he lost any more money, didn't you," Sheila said, laughing.

Karen laughed with her and changed the phone from her left ear to the right. "I did not."

"Yes, you did. Girl, I know you better than you know yourself."

Actually, Sheila did know her pretty well, but Karen had no idea why, because Lord knows their personalities were as different as June and December.

Karen was about to ask Sheila how the kids were doing, but she paused when she thought she heard a deep, heavy voice in the background. She just knew it wasn't Terrance's no-good ass. "Who is that talking to the kids?"

"All you're going to do is get mad, so I'm not even going to tell you."

Sheila was right, because Karen was already scowling.

"Why is it that Terrance always spends the entire day with you when you get your check but only shows up long enough for you to spread your legs during the rest of the month?"

"Look, Karen. I can't believe you even went there. I love Terrance, and whether you believe it or not, he loves me."

Love? Oh, now she understood. It must have been love he was showing her when he'd knocked up Sheila and two other women at the same time. Little William was probably the only kid around who had two half brothers the same age as he was. "Whatever, Sheila. I don't feel like arguing with you about this tired situation again, so I'll talk to you later. Okay?"

"See ya." Click.

Sheila was pissed.

Karen couldn't believe that girl. Here she was, twenty-eight, on welfare, a resident of one of the Housing Authority's worst projects, and yes, after eight long years, still screwing the same irresponsible, unemployed asshole that never gave her one dime to support his children. Karen loved her sister, but, damn, how stupid could one woman be? The idea of taking college courses or getting a job never seemed to enter her mind, and whenever Karen suggested it, all she would say was, "Girl, I've got to raise my children, and I can't do that from some penny-ante job or some boring classroom." As far as she was concerned, she didn't have to lift a finger until her children were completely grown, which would be a long time from now, since Shaniqua was the oldest and had just turned eight. It was a miracle how that poor little thing was a straight-A student, considering her household environment. Then there was Jason, who was six going on twenty-five. Just last week his first-grade teacher had told him to go sit down at his desk, but instead, he'd grabbed the little thing between his legs and told her to "get up on it." But had Sheila chewed his little butt out, or put him on punishment? Or better yet, whipped his little behind? Of course not. All she'd said was, "Jason, you know better than that." The woman obviously needed to be admitted somewhere, because any mother who would say some lame mess like that about something that serious couldn't possibly have it all upstairs.

Then there was three-year-old William, who could perfectly pronounce the words *shit*, *damn*, and *fuck* but had a blank look on his face when it was time for him to recite his ABCs. At the rate he was going, he'd be lucky if he passed kindergarten.

Dwelling on her sister's situation always pissed Karen off. She was sick and tired of giving Sheila money for food and buying clothes for her pitiful niece and two nephews. Hell, she didn't even have any children of her own, and here she was satisfying the responsibility of some deadbeat father who clearly didn't give a damn.

Karen picked up the cordless phone again and punched in her mother's phone number.

"Hello," Lucinda answered.

"Hey, Mom, how are you doing?"

"I'm fine. Richard and I were just sitting here watching *The Fresh Prince of Bel-Air*. What are you and John doing?"

"John is out getting a pizza, and I just finished talking to Sheila."

"I haven't heard from that girl in over a week."

"She said she hadn't talked to you today, but she didn't say it had been a whole week."

"What was she up to when you called her? Were the kids okay?"

"I guess they were doing fine, but I really didn't get a chance to ask her. She got highly upset because I made some comments about Terrance being at her apartment."

"She got her check today, didn't she?"

"You know she did, or he wouldn't have had his butt over there."

"Mmm, mmm, mmm. It's just a crying shame how she lets that boy use her like that. I wish that girl would open her eyes. I've talked to her over and over again, but she just won't listen. I don't know what else to do."

"Well, Mom, I know that's your baby girl, but you've got to stop worrying yourself about her. I'm starting to accept the fact that you can't make a grown person do anything they don't want to do, and I'm leaving it alone from here on out. All we can do now is pray about it."

"I've been doing that all along. I just hope our prayers are answered before she messes around and gets herself pregnant again."

"I know, Ma, but there's nothing we can do if she

won't listen to us. Well, I know you have company, but I just wanted to call and check on you, since I didn't get to talk to you too long this morning when I was at work. Tell Richard I said hi."

"I will. You tell John I said hello, and I love both of you."

"We love you too, Mom. I'll call you either tomorrow or Wednesday."

Karen was glad her mother had found a good man like Richard, and it put her mind at ease knowing he was there by Lucinda's side. She deserved someone like him. The man treated her with more love and respect than any woman could ever hope for and was like a second father to Karen. He'd asked Lucinda more than once to be his wife, but she had never agreed to it. And Karen knew it was only because she was terribly afraid of being hurt again. The same way she had been hurt by her first husband, Karen's father.

John put the pizza on the kitchen counter, removed his stone-washed jacket, and threw it on the chair closest to the sink. Karen was sitting at the one adjacent, watching him.

"Don't worry, I'm not gonna leave it lying there. I'm taking it upstairs as soon as I finish eating."

Karen had heard comments like that a hundred times. "What took you so long?" she asked.

"Nothing. I wasn't gone that long, was I?"

Karen reached over to the drawer, pulled out a miniature-sized steak knife and separated two slices of pizza. "No, but it doesn't take forty-five minutes to drive over to Golf Road."

"It couldn't have taken me that long," John said with a smirky grin on his face.

"You went to some convenience store to play the lottery, didn't you?"

"I won't even deny it, baby. I've got a good feeling about that Little Lotto tonight, and I only played five dollars."

Karen picked off each piece of pepperoni and set it to the edge of the pizza box. Cheese and sausage were more than enough for her. "That's five dollars you'd still have if you hadn't gambled it away. You're never going to learn, are you?"

John smiled with a mouth full of pizza. "Don't be mad. It's only the lottery, and you've got my promise about not going back to the track."

Karen didn't like this at all, but she genuinely understood how hard it was going cold turkey. It had taken her three months to give up chocolate muffins and sixty days more before she'd successfully weaned herself off those sinful Twix bars. But then, gaining weight and losing bill money were hardly one and the same. There was a lot more at risk with the latter, and that meant she had to get down on her knees and pray more this week than she had in a long time. Faith was the only chance she had with this gambling situation, and it was time for her to start acting like it. She hadn't been to church in a long time, not because she'd become some horrible, backsliding sinner, but mostly because she was too lazy to get all doodied up, especially since she was already having to do that five other days in the week. The Sabbath day had become her rest day, and she felt guilty. It seemed as though this problem she and John were having was God's way of reminding her that she needed to be prayerful at all times and not just when things were heading for destruction. Her grandma Claire used to say, "Get down on your knees and pray, even if it's just to give the Lord thanks." And starting tonight, that's exactly what she was going to do.

CHAPTER 6

"I 'LL HAVE A half-pound cheeseburger, small fries, and large Coke," Larry said. Regina had just ordered a grilled chicken sandwich and a medium pink lemonade. It was the quarter-pound burger that she wanted, but she'd decided against it. She'd made entirely too much progress with this weight thing to fall off the wagon now.

Regina made her way to the other end of Fuddruckers, a popular restaurant located right in the heart of Schaumburg, and secured a table, while Larry stood at the pop machine filling their cups with drinks. Afterward, he walked over to their table and seated himself directly across from Regina. Usually he sat kitty-corner from her whenever they ate out, wanting to be close to her, but not today. Maybe there was no substance to her thinking, but she was starting to feel paranoid again. He'd seemed so distant lately, as if he didn't enjoy being in her company. And yesterday, he'd phoned her at the last minute to cancel lunch, claiming his Monday morning staff meeting was going to run into his lunch hour.

"So, how's your day going?" Regina asked.

"Busy, but fine. I really should be working instead of having lunch, but I knew how much you were looking forward to this."

Damn. He was sounding like he'd been forced there against his precious little will. "Well, if you were that busy, you shouldn't have come. All you had to do was tell me," Regina said with a bit of salt in her voice.

Larry took a sip from his cola. "So you could accuse me of God knows what? Listen to you. You've got an attitude already."

Regina reached across the table and grabbed Larry's hand. Her feelings were clearly hurt, but she was hiding it well. "Let's not argue. Okay? I know you're busy, and I'm sorry for pressuring you about it."

He let out a sigh and turned his head toward the window. Why couldn't he look her straight in the eye? Her mother always said that when a person shied away from direct eye contact, it usually meant they were guilty of something. She hoped that wasn't Larry's case.

"So when do you plan on recruiting those supervisors you talked about over the weekend?" Regina asked, trying to smooth things over.

"When I met with two of the other division managers

yesterday, we thought we'd be able to start interviewing by next week, but I just found out today that I'll be down at our training facility in Atlanta for five days."

"Atlanta? When do you leave?"

"Probably Sunday evening, since the training session begins first thing Monday morning."

"Maybe I could take a vacation week and join you. We haven't gone away one single time this year, and you know how much I love Atlanta." She was excited.

They had gone there during their engagement and were absolutely impressed. Atlanta was a big city and just as exciting as Chicago but not nearly as congested. Down there, it was common to find successful black families living in two- and three-hundred-thousand dollar houses. As a matter of fact, entire subdivisions of them. Something that was basically foreign to most other areas of the country.

"I'll be in training every day from nine to four-thirty, so we wouldn't be able to spend any real time together. It wouldn't be much of a vacation for you at all, the way I see it."

What was he talking about? That was the same reason he hadn't wanted her to go with him to Philadelphia in January or to D.C. just over a month ago. Whether he was in training all day or not, how could she not have a good time in Atlanta, Georgia? "That's not a problem. I can find things to do during the day and spend time with you in the evening."

"Why don't you wait until July for the New Orleans

conference? It's only two months away, and it'll be easier for me to skip out on some of the workshops. I mean, I just can't see you wasting a whole week of your vacation when all you'd be doing is spending it alone."

"Then what if I just take off a couple of days and fly down on Thursday? That way we can stay on through Sunday."

"Four days won't be a vacation at all. If you wait until July, like I keep suggesting, we'll have an entire week."

Obviously, he wasn't going to budge. Why was he trying to sell her on this New Orleans trip, anyway? It just didn't make any sense. Regina thought the Quarters were nice and all, but girlfriend was rearing to go to Atlanta. Especially now, when the only weather Illinois was experiencing was constant rain, day after day, week after week.

Regina was about to take one more stand on this vacation issue when she noticed a look of frustration on Larry's face. "Fine. I'll wait until July, if you think it's best."

"I really do. We'll have a much better time. Just wait and see."

Better time? How? By July, the temperatures in the South would be so unbearable, that all they would be able to do was lie in some hotel suite trying their best to stay cool.

Regina looked at her watch. Shoot. She only had fifteen minutes to make it back to work, and the drive to Hoffman Estates would take no less than twenty. Normally, she could be a little late returning from lunch, but today she'd scheduled an interview right at one-thirty, and it was unprofessional to keep someone waiting. Especially when that someone was a top female engineering graduate from Yale University.

At the request of Regina's boss, the vice president of Human Resources, she had tried to recruit this young, Asian woman before but had been unsuccessful due to the woman's salary and perk requirements. The offer would be more to her liking this time, though. Regina was going to see to it.

"I really hate to cut this short, but I need to get back. I've got an appointment this afternoon," she said, then patted her lips with her napkin.

Larry slid his chair back from the table, stood up, and buttoned his blazer. "I've got to get going myself."

Regina took out her bronze-colored Fashion Fair lipstick and ran it across her lips. She stood up, and they walked toward the exit. Larry grabbed her by her waist as they started toward their respective cars.

He walked over to Regina's car, opened the door on the driver's side, and waited for her to get in. "I hope you're not disappointed about Atlanta. New Orleans is a much better idea. You'll see."

Yeah, she was going to see all right. See him down in Atlanta next week.

REGINA PUSHED her office door shut, walked across the teal plush carpet, and sat down. The interview had gone well. The electrical engineering managerial position was finally filled, and the young woman was starting at the end of the month. As anticipated, the salary issue had come up, but shortly after Regina had disclosed an offer of $85,000 per year, the engineering graduate had quickly accepted and suddenly had had no further questions. It just went to show, money didn't mean everything, but it certainly came pretty damn close.

Regina glanced over at her wedding photo and smiled. She and Larry looked good together, were the perfect couple, and that's how it was going to stay. Regina was going to use everything in her power to transform this Atlanta business trip into a second honeymoon. Of course Larry was against the idea right now, but his feelings would be different once she got down there.

She reached for the phone at the edge of her desk and called Larry's office. Doris, his secretary, would have his complete travel itinerary and would gladly aid her in modifying his hotel reservations.

"Larry Moore's office," a woman said.

Who was this answering the phone? Doris was middle-aged and Caucasian, but this particular voice belonged to a sister. As far as she knew, there were no African-American secretaries in Larry's department, but then, maybe they had hired one and he'd just forgotten to mention it. "Is this Larry Moore's office?" Regina asked, then realized how stupid she sounded, since the woman had already announced that it was.

"Yes, it is."

"Actually, I'm looking for his secretary. Is she in?"

"Yes. May I tell her who's calling?"

"This is Mrs. Moore."

"Please hold."

Regina leaned back, rested her elbows on each arm of the chair, and waited.

"This is Doris. May I help you?"

"Hey, Doris, it's Regina."

"Hi, Regina. How are you? You just missed Larry."

Doris spoke fast and to the point but, as always, with a pleasant tone of voice. Which is why Regina loved talking to her. "As a matter of fact, I was calling for you. I need to find out which hotel Larry is staying at in Atlanta, so I can extend the reservations through Sunday. I'm planning to fly down there and surprise him on next Thursday."

"Well, good for you. Now let me see here . . . he's staying at the Marriott Marquis."

"Good. That's a supernice hotel. We stayed there last year and loved it."

"I remember Larry talking about it when you guys got back. Have you made your flight reservations yet?"

"No. He just told me about the trip at lunchtime, and I'm just now getting an opportunity to make a few phone calls."

"I can call and book it for you, if you want."

Regina smiled. It was just like Doris to offer to help someone else. "I don't want to bother you with that, and anyway, I can make one phone call to the corporate travel division here at my company and they'll take care of everything. But thanks for offering."

"Okay, but you know it wouldn't be a problem."

"While you're worrying about me, you should be planning your own vacation," Regina said and then laughed.

"Actually, I'm training someone right now, because I'll be leaving day after tomorrow for two weeks. My husband and I are flying out to California to visit my daughter and son-in-law."

Well, that explained why the sister had answered the phone. She was probably from one of those temporary agencies.

"I'm really glad to hear you're taking a break, because I know how busy you guys have been," Regina said.

"Yeah, we were flooded with work in January, but things have been pretty slow since then. To tell you the truth, I'm glad, because this way I won't have to worry about getting so far behind in my work while I'm gone."

Slow? Since January? Hell, that was three months ago. If they were so slow, why did Larry keep insisting he needed to work through lunch and after normal working hours? She didn't understand and wanted more information, but she didn't want Doris to know what she was thinking.

"Well, if I don't talk with you before you leave, have a safe and enjoyable trip," Regina said.

"We will, and you do the same. I can just see the look on Larry's face now. He'll be so surprised."

"Thanks again, Doris."

"You're welcome, Regina. Good-bye."

Regina placed the phone on its ivory-colored base, kicked her black pumps under her desk, and discharged a deep sigh. For every bright side she tried to look on, there was a dark and gloomy one peeking around the corner. She was trying so hard to understand Larry. Trying to make him happy. But now he was lying.

First it was the working through lunch hour thing, then came the working after hours, and now it was these Friday night card game extravaganzas. Before long, he'd have an excuse for not coming home at all.

She sat in her chair with her eyes shut and tried to calm herself down. Maybe her imagination was out of control again, the same way it had been on Friday night. And anyway, it didn't automatically mean Larry's work-load was down just because Doris's was. He was a manager with a lot more responsibility and really couldn't be compared with his secretary.

Once again she convinced herself. If Larry said he had a lot of work, then he did. She had always been able to trust him in the past, and now was no different. He'd always been a dedicated employee, and she was foolish for thinking anything else. She told herself that everything was fine.

REGINA HADN'T WANTED to go shopping alone, and since Karen and John had already made plans for the evening, she phoned Marilyn and asked her to meet her at the mall right after work. She wouldn't be leaving for Atlanta for another week, but she wanted to get a head start on buying some new apparel for the trip. They'd already browsed through two major department stores but, for some reason, hadn't found anything worth writing home about. Finally, they'd decided to check out Nordstrom's lingerie department.

"Girl, I know you're not serious about spending sixty dollars on that skimpy little nightgown," Marilyn said. "You must be out of your mind."

"Actually, sixty dollars isn't a whole lot for this, because I've seen some a lot higher than that," Regina said.

"That's just plain ridiculous. You would never catch me spending that type of money on something like that. Even if I had the money to do it."

Regina carried the flame red negligee around to the other side of the rack so she could pick out a silk robe to match it. "Larry and I haven't gone away together since last year, and I want to make this Atlanta trip as special as I can. Sometimes you have to add some spice to a marriage so it won't become so monotonous. Besides, I haven't charged anything on my Nordstrom account in over two months, so it really doesn't matter how much it costs."

"What difference does that make? You still have to pay for it one way or the other. Not to mention those ridiculous finance charges you'll be stuck with."

"But I won't have to pay for it all at once, and that's what makes the difference as far as I'm concerned."

"I guess, but I still think it's priced way too high. There's just no way I could fork out that kind of money for something you can't even wear outside of a bedroom. But then, it's your money."

Exactly, Regina thought. And as long as Marilyn wasn't spending any of her precious little money, she shouldn't be worrying about how much it cost in the first place. Marilyn sure was being overly critical tonight. Maybe she was just having a bad day, but Regina wished she would cut it out. "You should be buying one yourself. You never know when Mr. Right might come along."

"Girl, please. It's like I told you a couple of days ago, that's never going to happen."

"Don't be so negative. I mean, look at me, I found the perfect husband two years ago, but before I met Larry, I had the same attitude you've got right now. You just have to have a little faith is all."

"I've had faith all along, but as you can see, it hasn't gotten me anywhere. You're just one of the lucky ones. There aren't a lot of Larrys out there."

Regina spotted a paisley robe with mixtures of red in it and pulled it off the rack. "Yeah, I am blessed to have a good husband, but I can't believe he's the only one. As a matter of fact, I know he's not the only one, because John is definitely the ideal husband. Karen couldn't have made a better choice if she had planned it."

"And I'll bet that's the only other man you can think of, too."

"You just have to be patient. If I'd rushed into marrying someone that wasn't right for me, there's no telling what I might be going through right now." Regina glanced at her watch and saw that it was a few minutes past seven-thirty. "Girl, I didn't know we'd been in here this long. I wanted to get this stuff home and put away before Larry made it back, but by now, I'm sure he's already gotten there. There's no way I can let him see any of this, because he knows I only buy outfits like this when I'm planning to go away somewhere."

"Just tell him you were out shopping. He doesn't have to know what for, and all you have to do is throw the stuff in the trunk until tomorrow."

"Yeah, I guess that's the only choice I have anyway. I'm going over to the checkout counter, so I can get everything rung up. But you can keep looking around if you want to."

"I'll be over in the shoe department. Just come over there when you're finished, and then we'll leave."

Regina passed her selections over to the smiling, blond cashier and watched her scan each of the price tags. Her situation wasn't as bad as she'd thought. Nothing was like being alone and trying unsuccessfully to find the right man to settle down with. She felt sorry for Marilyn. And one thing was for sure, she wasn't about to go back to living her life like that. All she needed to do was put some fire back into her marriage. And this "skimpy little nightgown" was going to help her do just that.

CHAPTER 7

I
T WAS ALREADY 8 A.M but Regina was still rushing around the bedroom trying frantically to finish packing. She couldn't believe it had only been a week and a half ago that Larry had first told her about his business trip. Her plane was leaving at noon and she wanted to be at the airport at least ninety minutes earlier. Now, she wished she'd taken one of the later flights. But at the time, it just hadn't seemed logical to spend two hundred dollars more when all she really had to do was get her lazy butt up a little earlier than usual. Not to mention the fact that she would've had to hear Larry throwing a pissy fit when he received the American Express statement at the end of next month.

She unzipped the garment bag hanging on the bedroom door, walked into the closet, and took down the items she'd picked up from the cleaners two days ago: a sleeveless red linen dress, a medium blue after-five pantsuit, and an off-white London Fog trench, just in case it got cool.

Next, she removed the shorts set she'd purchased last year from Lord & Taylor's end-of-the-season sale. Usually, she took twice as many clothes as she needed, but she didn't see a reason to do that this time. All she was going to need for this particular weekend were the three nighties lying over there on the edge of the bed.

She picked up the black lacey one, folded it, and placed it neatly inside the left end of the suitcase. She did the same with the purple one. Then, she scooped up the red satin one. It was more beautiful now than it had been in the store. Hmmph. She didn't care what Miss Marilyn had thought about the big price tag. Larry was going to flip when he saw her in this, and that was the only thing that counted.

She tucked the last piece of underwear inside the suitcase and was starting toward the brass vanity set when the phone rang.

"Hello?" Regina said.

"Hi, baby."

Uh-oh. Why was Larry calling her at home when he knew she was supposed to be at work? Since Atlanta's time zone was an hour ahead of Schaumburg's, he should've already been in class by now. What was she going to do? Better than that, what was she going to say? She'd done everything in her power to keep her plans undercover, and there was no way she was going to blow it now. She had to think fast.

"Hi. How'd you know I was home?"

"I called your office, but when I got your voice mail message, I pressed zero and spoke with your secretary. What are you doing at home? It's after eight o'clock there, isn't it?"

Regina paused so she could gather her thoughts and tiny white lies together. "No, I'm just running a little late. I'll get there by nine, though. Aren't you supposed to be in class?"

"Actually, I am, but I wanted to call you before I went in. I really wish you had come down here. We could have had a great time, and you don't know how sorry I am for talking you out of it."

She was about to burst. She wanted to spill her guts and let him know that he hadn't talked her out of it. That she had made plane reservations. That she had extended his hotel stay. That she would be there by this afternoon. But she just couldn't do that.

"I tried to tell you that it would've been a nice vacation for us, but you wouldn't listen. As a matter of fact, you haven't been listening to much of anything I have to say lately. But then you know what they say."

"No, what's that?"

"Absence makes the heart grow fonder. And maybe that's what's happening to you."

"All I know is that I miss you a lot, and I can't wait until I get home tomorrow evening, so I can hold you, kiss you, and make love to you until I'm completely worn out."

Shoot, he was getting his chance to do that tonight. He just didn't know it yet. "I miss you too, Larry. More than you'll ever know. I know we've been arguing a lot, but I'm confident that things will get better between us. Maybe all we needed was some time apart."

"What? Did you say 'time apart'? I can't believe I'm hearing that from the woman who wants to monitor my every move and gets highly upset when I don't spend all of my free time with her," Larry said and cracked up laughing.

"I'm only like that because I love you so much, and I don't want to be without you. But, I admit, maybe I have been being a little too tight with you, and I'm going to work on that from here on out."

"You don't know how much of a relief it is to hear you say that. Well it's after nine, so I better mosey on into the conference room before they send out a search party. I'll give you a call tonight after dinner, though. Okay?"

"Sounds good. I love you, Larry."

"I love you, too, baby. Bye."

Regina was grinning from ear to ear. Larry was missing her more than she'd thought. How could she have ever doubted a man like this? She was glad she'd followed her first instinct and was flying down to Georgia. This was going to be one of the best trips they'd ever had, and just thinking about it caused her heart to race.

She started for the vanity set again, but this time the doorbell rang.

Damn. Now what? The clock was already pushing eight-thirty, and she didn't have time for any more of these interruptions. Who could it be, anyway? Both Karen and Marilyn were probably already at work by now, and it was way too early for any Jehovah's Witnesses to be out canvassing the subdivision, knocking on every door.

She made her way down to the main floor and over to the living room window. When she looked out, she saw Karen preparing to ring the doorbell again.

"Girl, what are you doing here? You're supposed to be at work, aren't you?" Regina asked and stepped aside so Karen could walk in.

"You know I am, but I wanted to stop by and see you before you left. John and I have been so tied up this week, and I feel bad about not being able to talk to you as much as I usually do. Especially since I know how lonely you get when Larry is on those business trips."

"Girl, don't worry about that. I'm just glad you and John have worked out your differences, because that's more important than anything. I knew he was just going through a phase."

"I know, but you're the closest friend I have, and I want you to know I'm here for you whenever you need me. You know how upset you got with me when John and I first met. Remember when I wasn't calling you or coming by as much?"

"Please. That was five years ago, and all I was doing back then was being selfish, because I didn't have any-body to settle down with myself."

"Still, I don't want you to think I'm not here for you."

"Girl, I never think anything like that. You've been the one person in my life that I've always been able to depend on. If anything, I'm the one who should be feeling guilty. I won't even be here for your birthday tomorrow."

"It's not really a big deal. I'm only turning thirty."

"It's a big deal to me, because now you're over the hill like the rest of us, and those twenties are long gone forever," Regina said.

"Girl, shut up. Don't you have some packing to finish?" Karen said, laughing.

"As a matter of fact I do, and since you're so broken up about not being here for me, you can come on up here and help me take care of it," Regina said and started up the stairs.

Karen dropped her purse down on the sofa and followed behind her. "I hope you're not taking your entire wardrobe like you usually do when you go out of town. You're only going to be gone four days."

"Actually, I toned it down a lot this time, because I'm hoping I won't have to wear any clothing on this trip."

"Well, I guess I heard that. You must be planning to whip Kitty on him in a big way this weekend."

"Shoot, I haven't had any since he left on Sunday, and right now, I'm fiending for d-i-c-k like a drug addict gone without crack."

"You are so sick," Karen said, laughing. "Shoot, in our household, John is the sex maniac. That man thinks it's normal procedure to have sex twice a day, seven days a week, and gets an attitude if I even act like I'm tired or don't feel like it. I've told him over and over how statistics show that most married couples only have sex two to three times a week, but all he has to say to that is, 'We're not like most married couples.' This morning, after the alarm went off, he sat up in bed and didn't move for a whole minute. I knew what he was waiting for, so I pretended to be asleep. Of course, he kept calling my name and shaking my arm until finally, I had no choice but to open my eyes. 'Karen. Karen. Karen. Can I have some lovin' before I get in the shower?' "

Regina placed the last toiletry into the overnight bag and said, "Well?"

"Well, what?"

"Did you give him some or didn't you? Inquiring minds want to know."

Karen sat down on the bed and laughed. "If you must know, yes, I did go ahead and give him some. I didn't feel like it, but since he's finally given up this gambling thing, I figure the least I can do is try and satisfy his other obsession."

"You ought to be thankful that you have a man who desires you every day. Shit, if Larry wanted to make love as often as John does, I wouldn't hardly be complaining. I'd be in hog heaven."

"I'll just bet you would. Girl, you've been craving sex ever since I can remember. I don't know how Larry puts up with your hot self. Twenty years from now, he'll probably have a heart attack right on top of your ass, if not before."

"Please. He can take it, and if there ever comes a time when he can't, he'd better be figuring out real quick what to do about it, because I'll be wanting sex long after I'm some fifty years old."

"Girl, while you're going on and on about your favorite pastime, you'd better be getting the last of your things into that garment bag. What time did you say you had to be at the airport?"

"Twelve," Regina said after glancing over at the clock radio on the nightstand. "I want to be out of here by nine-thirty, though."

"Yeah, that's probably a good idea, since you know how congested O'Hare can be. If you need me to drop you off, I can. All I have to do is call my boss and let him know I need to take a half day of vacation. I'm going to have to take a couple hours of personal time for this morning, anyhow."

"No, but thanks for offering. Larry and I won't be back in Chicago until around ten or so on Sunday night, and I don't want to bother anyone to come pick us up. Plus, I think it only costs about twelve dollars a day to leave the car at the terminal."

"Only? I'm glad you've got forty-eight dollars to throw away, because I sure don't. There is no way I would spend that kind of money if I knew someone was willing to drop me off and pick me up."

"You're starting to sound the same way Marilyn did last week when we were at the mall."

"That's a scary thought. What did she say to criticize you this time?"

"Well, it wasn't so much that she was criticizing me, at least not directly, but she was pretty upset at the fact that I spent sixty dollars on this red nightgown," Regina said, slipping it out of the suitcase and passing it over to Karen.

"This is beautiful, but, as much as I hate to agree with any of what Miss Thing has to say, I have to agree that sixty dollars was a bit steep for any piece of lingerie I can think of. Especially since you probably won't have it on longer than five minutes."

"Maybe so, but I don't care if I only get to wear it for two minutes, just so long as it turns Larry on. When he called earlier, all he talked about was how he wished I had flown down to Atlanta, and how he couldn't wait to get home and make love to me. And this outfit right here is going to make him want to even more."

"You don't have to convince me. It's your pocketbook, and you know we never see eye to eye when it comes to money, anyway, so there's no sense in us going round and round about something that we're never going to agree on."

"You're sounding like Marilyn again. You guys are just too conservative. Shit, you only live once, and as far as I'm concerned, there's no guarantee that tomorrow will even come."

Karen didn't say anything, because it was that very attitude that caused Regina and Larry to live from week to week and the reason Regina was always having to worry about which bill she was going to be able to put off until next month. Which never made any sense, because if she didn't have enough money to pay it this month, how was she going to pay twice as much the next? Regina was Karen's best friend, but how anybody with a household income over one hundred thousand dollars could position themselves into a financial situation like that was far beyond Karen.

Regina tucked the expensive nightgown back into the suitcase. "Well, I guess that's about it. All I have to do now is slip on my jeans, put on my face, and brush through my hair."

"I'll zip up all your luggage and take it down to the living room while you're doing that," Karen said and stood up. "Is there anything else you want me to do?"

"No, I think that's it." Regina sashayed into the bathroom off the master bedroom.

Karen zipped both the garment and overnight bags and then the medium-sized suitcase. She carried them down to the living room all at once and then returned up to the bedroom. She leaned her shoulder inside the bathroom doorway and watched Regina smooth on her foundation. "I can't believe Larry didn't find out about you coming down there or at least get a little suspicious at some point."

Regina went across her right eyelash with brownish-black mascara. "I really think he believed I was sold on that New Orleans trip in July. Although, I was so afraid that he had busted me this morning when he called and realized I wasn't at work, but I played it off as best I could. It didn't sound like he suspected anything out of the ordinary."

"How did he know you were at home in the first place?"

"He called my office, and when Shelly told him I wasn't in yet, he called here. I didn't think he would call me at work, since he'd been calling every night, and it was a good thing I'd warned her of what to say just in case."

Karen folded her arms, leaned her head against the doorway, and yawned. "I'm so tired, and I'm starting to feel sleepy."

"If my husband had jumped my bones last night and then again first thing this morning, I would be tired and sleepy too."

"Is your mind ever out of the gutter?" Karen said, shaking her head.

"Well, you know that's what it is, unless maybe you're pregnant."

"Girl, please. Don't even wish something that terrible on me, unless you want to see me totally lose my mind and slip into a severe state of depression. It's almost nine-thirty, so you better get your butt out of that mirror before you miss your flight," Karen said and then walked over to the chaise and lay back on it.

Regina was still laughing. "I knew if I brought up the subject of having babies, you'd wake up in a heartbeat."

CHAPTER 8

R EGINA HAD made it to Atlanta. Finally, all the sneak-
ing, planning, and shopping for this major event were
now only minutes away from paying off. This was
going to be the surprise of Larry's life, and she couldn't
wait to see his reaction. He'd be shocked at first but even-
tually overjoyed.

The plane ride hadn't been the greatest, though. The
flight had been delayed two hours because of some
maintenance problem, and her ears were still plugged
from all the popping. What's more, she still had that
woozy feeling in her stomach that had come right when
the pilot had reached cruising altitude. Her nerves were
running wild from all of the excitement, and her heart
was beating a mile a minute.

She couldn't wait to see her husband, and this taxi
driver wasn't going nearly as fast as she needed him to.

She wanted him to ride in the backseat so she could take over the steering wheel. She would show him how to get there in what Karen's grandmother used to call "a who run and a rip." Regina smiled, because Grandma Claire had always had a funny and unique way with words. Words Regina had never heard anywhere else. Like "she-booty," which meant a "big behind." Or "jessey," which meant "just any kind." Or "jack leg," which was a minister who was sure he could, but didn't know how to, preach. And best of all was "cuff," which was an outrageous black person that had no morals. Regina could still hear Grandma Claire saying now, "Cuffs just won't act right." Karen was the only person she knew who had a grandmother so humorous, so wise and so loving.

But then, Karen always seemed to have the best of everything. It was Karen who had always been the teacher's pet. It was Karen who had always gotten the straight As in high school—without studying until the night before a test. It was Karen who, even without being light-skinned, had the clearest skin. It was Karen who'd always gotten the best-looking boyfriends. It was Karen who'd graduated magna cum laude from college and had completed her MBA while working full-time. It was Karen who'd been the first to find a husband that worshiped the ground that she walked on. It was Karen who had first moved into one of the ritziest subdivisions in the Northwest suburbs of Chicago. It was Karen who had first purchased an SUV. It was Karen who had been promoted twice in one year and received a huge raise.

Regina didn't know whether to be angry at herself or downright embarrassed because of what she was thinking. Karen was her best friend and had proven it over and over, time and time again. She'd had these thoughts a lot lately, though, and couldn't understand why. Surely, she didn't envy Karen. At least, she didn't think she did. And anyway, how could she? Karen was her girl. The sister she'd never had. They had played together as children and cried together whenever there was trouble. But it was just that everything always seemed to fall right down in her lap without her ever having to put forth any real effort to get it. Sometimes it just didn't seem fair.

Regina wished this driver would step on it. "How far are we from the Marriott?" she finally asked.

"It's just up ahead," the taxi driver said and pointed straight in front of him.

Good. She dug inside her purse, located her compact, removed her black Ray-Bans, and patted her nose with the pink, plush sponge. Her lipstick was still intact from when she'd freshened it up right after landing. She forced the compact back into her purse and pulled out her wallet so she'd be ready to pay the cab fare the moment they arrived in front of the hotel. When she started to put her sunglasses back on, she noticed the driver gaping at her in his rearview mirror. Admiring her, she guessed, and to tell the truth, she understood why. Luanne had outdone herself when she'd cut her hair two days ago, and Regina's complexion was completely blemish free, thanks to those Ambi skin-care products she'd been using religiously for the last two months. It may have been vain, but she knew she was looking good.

She scanned all of the buildings as they continued down the street. Peachtree Avenue sort of reminded her of Michigan Avenue in Chicago. Right in the heart of downtown and filled with clusters of stores and restaurants of all kinds. If it hadn't been for that plane delay, she would've had plenty of time to drop her luggage off at the front desk of the hotel and visit at least a couple of the clothing shops before Larry's class was over. She still needed to find Karen a birthday gift. But then, she would definitely have time tomorrow. All day, for that matter.

They rolled up in front of the hotel, and as planned, she handed the man a twenty-dollar bill, told him to keep the change, and swung open the car door. She pulled out the overnight bag, threw it on the same shoulder her purse was swinging from, retrieved the last two pieces of luggage from the backseat, and, although she didn't intend to, slammed the door.

Each of the bellboys standing out front were busy with other patrons, and she didn't have time for any more of this waiting. She proceeded toward the revolving door but then realized how impossible it was going to be to get through it, since she was carrying such a bulky load. She glanced to the right and spied a normal door, but just when she went to set down the suitcase to open it, a cute little Chinese boy did it for her. "Thank you," she said, smiling at him. She wasn't sure if he understood English or not, but when she saw him smile back as if acknowledging her appreciation, she figured he did.

She strode through the luxurious lobby toward the long row of elevators and pressed the top button. Just standing inside a hotel of this distinction gave her a cozy feeling. Made her feel important. And who wouldn't? The color scheme was a beautiful, deep shade of burgundy, and the atrium hovering over her was completely out of this world. Not to mention the more than sixteen hundred rooms spread throughout all forty-seven floors.

When she turned back toward the elevator, she heard a chime, and the door directly in front of her opened. A middle-aged black couple, a young black girl, probably their teenaged daughter, and an older, classy-looking white gentleman stepped out. Regina, two other women, and a bellboy stepped on.

"You've got quite a load. Which floor are you going to?" one of the women asked.

"Twenty-two, thank you," Regina said and smiled.

When they arrived at the tenth floor, the two women got off, and the bellboy did the same on the seventeenth. When the car reached the twenty-second floor, Regina stepped out, studied the arrows on the wall to see which direction room 2218 was in, and headed straight for it. Finally.

She positioned herself in front of Larry's room, dropped everything on the floor except her purse, and knocked three times. With all of the rushing and excitement, she hadn't even considered the fact that Larry might not even be in his room. She raised her right fist to knock again but lowered it when she heard footsteps approaching the door, which opened halfway.

"Just sit it down on the dresser," Larry said.

It was all Regina could do to keep from cracking up when she realized Larry had mistaken her for room service. She pushed the door open a little farther and saw him walking away. He was wearing the black terry-cloth wrap she'd bought for him last Christmas, and his body looked good enough to eat. She dragged her luggage inside, sat her purse down on top of it, and shut the door. She heard the shower running, and she was glad she'd gotten there in time enough to jump in with him. They hadn't made love under steamy, hot running water in a long time, and she was looking forward to it.

"I'm not room service, but I've got everything you need for dinner," she said, laughing.

Larry swirled around, looking as if he'd just seen a ghost.

"Aren't you going to say anything?" she asked.

"What are you doing here?" Larry finally asked.

"What do you think? To spend some time with my handsome husband."

He moved closer to her. "Why didn't you tell me you were coming when I called you this morning?"

Regina met him halfway and reached out to embrace him. "I wanted this to be a surprise, and it was more than worth it just to see this look on your face. I really got you good this time, didn't I?"

Larry wrapped his arms around her, still in a state of shock. "I really wish you'd told me, Regina."

She leaned her head back and stared him straight in his face. "Why? All that matters now is that I'm here, and now we can finally spend some quality time together in this gorgeous hotel suite."

Larry opened his mouth to say something, but just then the shower was turned off. Regina jerked her arms from around him.

"What happened to the shower? Why did it just shut off like that?" she asked.

"You really should have told me you were flying down here."

What the hell was he talking about? She had a feeling she didn't want to know. "Is somebody in there?"

Larry didn't say anything. Didn't even move.

"Why aren't you saying anything, Larry? What is going on here?" The tone of her voice was much louder now than it had been one minute ago.

Regina pushed past him, stormed into the next room where the king-sized bed was, and shoved open the bathroom door. Larry rushed behind her.

Regina's heart dropped through her stomach when she saw who was standing in front of the shower door reaching for a bath towel. This just couldn't be. She clinched her eyes shut and prayed this was nothing more than a dream, but when she opened them, Marilyn was still standing before her, butt naked and dripping wet. Regina felt as though she was being struck with high-voltage shock waves. Then with no warning and no energy to prevent it, she collapsed against the wall and slid all the way down. Tears were already flooding her cheeks. Larry pulled her up, into his arms, and escorted her back out to the bedroom. Marilyn stood in the same spot where she was, motionless.

When Regina realized Larry was holding her, she pushed him away and cried, "Why, Larry? How could you do something like this? Oh God, how could you do something like this?"

Larry held both hands up and opened his mouth, but nothing came out.

"How could you mess around with one of my closest friends?" Regina said, wiping her tears with her hands.

Larry inched a little closer to Regina. "Let me explain, Regina. It's not what you think. It's not what you think at all."

"I come in here and find Marilyn butt naked and you're telling me it's not what I think? Please. Larry, you must think I'm crazy."

Regina turned toward the bathroom and saw Marilyn coming out wearing a lavender silk robe. This bitch was bold. She wasn't making any attempt to get dressed or leave or do anything. Regina was boiling hot. "How could you do some shit like this, Marilyn? I've been a good friend to you for the last twelve years. I can't believe you would even stoop to some shit like this. What's the matter with you?"

"Look Regina, I'm sorry you had to find out like this, but

now that everything is all out in the open, none of us has to ride down front street anymore. I don't have to pretend that you and I are good friends, and Larry doesn't have to pretend that he loves you, when he knows he doesn't."

"What do you mean we're not friends? You know, Karen has been right about your critical, jealous, cheap-dressing, pony weave-wearing ass all along, and I was stupid for not listening to her. And I can't believe you had the audacity to go shopping with me last week, knowing good and well you were flying your ass down here. You wanted me to find out this way, and only a filthy, rotten bitch could do some shit like that."

Larry cocked his head to the side and then up the same way that ring-eyed dog on the *Little Rascals* used to do when he was totally surprised about something. He couldn't believe Marilyn had known all along that Regina was flying down to be with him. Damn. He'd been planning to tell Regina real soon, but not like this.

"Marilyn. I need to talk to Regina alone, so can you please get dressed and leave the room for a while?" Larry said and then took a deep breath.

"What do you need to talk to her alone for? She knows what's up now, and that's all she needs to know. If you think I'm going to leave her alone with you so she can beg and plead with you not to leave her, you must be crazy."

"Bitch, what do you mean *beg*? This is *my* husband, not yours," Regina yelled and then stepped so close to Marilyn that their bodies almost brushed.

"I mean exactly what I said, and as far as I can see, you're the only bitch in here. The man doesn't want you anymore, and begging is the only leg you've got to stand on."

Regina couldn't take this shit anymore, and before she knew it, she had hauled off and slapped Marilyn with her right hand. Marilyn grabbed the left side of her face, obviously trying to ease the pain, and then gazed at Regina with her eyes squinted. "It's on now, bitch," Marilyn said, swinging both her arms.

Larry jumped between the two of them, facing Marilyn and grabbing both of her hands before she could take a single strike at Regina. "Marilyn, please don't do this," Larry said.

"Move, Larry. Didn't you just see that bitch slap me?" Marilyn screamed.

Regina made her way around Larry and knocked Marilyn's head to the side as hard as she could with the flat of her hand. Marilyn broke away from Larry, turned around, and resumed swinging with all her might. Regina fought back. Their bodies locked together and collided against the wall, Regina pulling Marilyn's weave, hoping to yank it apart from the two inches of natural hair that she had, and Marilyn pressing Regina's face with as much force as she was capable of, trying hard to bruise it. Larry tried to pull them apart, but they were holding each other too tightly, and neither of them was willing to let go.

"Regina! Marilyn! Will you guys please stop this? This is so ridiculous," Larry said, sounding like a little wimp.

Larry made another brave attempt to separate them and finally succeeded. Marilyn stroked her hair down on both sides, checking to see if any was missing, and Regina stood where she was, eagerly awaiting round two.

"Marilyn, for the second time, can you please take your clothing into the bathroom and get dressed, so I can talk to Regina alone? That's the least you can do since you've caused all of this in the first place. It didn't have to turn out like this."

"Oh, so now I'm the cause of all this? Well, since that's the case, let me set the record straight. Is it my fault that you've been fucking me every Friday night for the last few weeks, when your wife thought your lying ass was out playing cards? Was it my idea to go on your last two business trips? Was it my fault every time you lied to your wife about working all that overtime when all the time you were at my place, lying up in my bed doing the wild thing? Was it my idea to call your house and hang up whenever Regina answered? Was it my fault when you pretended it was just an obscene phone call whenever I called and you answered and Regina was sitting right in front of you?" Marilyn waited for Larry's response.

He didn't as much as grunt.

"Oh, I guess you don't have anything to say now, right?" Marilyn asked and then picked up her black silk blouse and black dress pants. "Letting your little head think for your big one is what caused all of this. Make no mistake about that." Marilyn waltzed into the bathroom and slammed the door behind her.

Larry glanced over at Regina and regretted it. How was he going to explain any of this to a woman who looked like she was ready to contend with Mike Tyson? Her hair was scattered all over her head, her mascara was smeared, and her clothes were wrinkled to no end. "I'm really sorry things turned out like this, Regina. I mean, you've got to believe me, I never meant for you to find out like this, and if I had only known you were coming down here, this never would have happened."

Regina walked in front of Larry. "So now it's my fault, too, I guess? And in case you've forgotten, let me refresh your memory: We're married, Larry. I shouldn't have had to warn you or tell you about anything, and if you were a faithful husband, the way any married man should be, none of this would be happening. I still can't believe you've been doing this to me all this time. I mean, that slut is right there in the next room, and I still can't believe this shit." Regina went over to the edge of the bed on the far side and dropped down on it.

"All I can say is that I'm sorry," Larry muttered. "This got way out of hand, and I didn't mean for it to turn out like this. I have way more respect for you than that."

Regina turned away from Larry, retrieved a couple of tissues from the box sitting on the nightstand, and wiped her eyes and face. "Respect? What the fuck do you know about respect? Obviously, not a got-damn thing."

Marilyn jerked open the bathroom door, stampeded through to the living area, snatched up her non-designer, probably-not-genuine leather purse from the chair, and opened the door leading to the hallway. "I'm giving your ass one hour, Larry, and that's it," Marilyn said, strutting out the door without closing it.

"You black bitch," Regina yelled out to Marilyn.

Marilyn stepped back in front of the doorway. "What did you call me?"

"You heard me."

Marilyn came back into the room and was heading toward Regina when Larry moved in front of her. Without any argument, she rolled her eyes at Regina and then walked out the door again.

"Damn," Regina said. "That bitch is acting like she's got papers on you."

Larry walked over to shut the door, but when he saw the guy from room service rolling up with the food cart, he pulled it farther open instead.

"You can set it on the dresser," Larry said.

"All you need to do is sign at the bottom," the hotel employee said, handing him the ticket and pen.

Larry signed it, handed it back to him, and the guy from room service left. Larry eased the door shut.

"Can you wait until I throw some clothes on?" he said to Regina. "I promise, it won't take a minute."

Shit, that was the least he could do. All this parading around with hardly anything on reminded her of what he was about to do right before she'd busted his no-good ass, and to tell the truth, she was sick of it. "Go ahead, because I'm not going anywhere until you explain every inch of this shit to me." Regina stood up, went into the other room, and sat down on the multi-colored sofa.

She couldn't help replaying everything that Marilyn had just said, but the two business trips stuck out in her mind the most. How could she have been so stupid? When Larry had gone to Philadelphia in January, Marilyn had supposedly been at an annual seminar that her company had sent her to, and when he'd made the trip to D.C. back in March, Marilyn had claimed she was going home to Cincinnati to visit her parents. She had looked Regina straight in her face both times and lied. Come to think of it, Regina had helped her pack for both of those trips and had checked on her condo for her while she was gone. "What a sick and immoral bitch," Regina said out loud before she realized it.

After a few minutes passed, Larry made his way back to the front room with his tail between his legs and sat down next to Regina. "Things have been going bad between us for some time now, and although I know it's not right, I started seeing Marilyn. It wasn't planned, it just happened."

"How does some shit like this just happen, Larry? Are you in love with her? Do you plan on spending the rest of your life with her? Do you want a divorce? What?"

"I don't know, I mean I just don't know," Larry said and buried his face in the palms of his hands.

"What do you mean, you don't know? How can you not know?"

"I just don't know."

Damn. Actually, she was being sarcastic when she'd asked him about wanting a divorce, but the man was sounding like it was a serious possibility. "You know, Larry, the thing that pisses me off the most is that you didn't have the decency to tell me before now. I gave your tired ass plenty of opportunities to 'fess up, but you chose to keep lying to me. I've been asking you on and off over the last few weeks if there was someone else, and you kept saying you didn't want anybody else, that you loved me, that I was blowing everything out of proportion, that I was being too tight on you . . . and the list goes on. How come you couldn't just be a man and admit that you were screwing some whore I've been friends with for more than a decade? Shit, I'm the one that introduced the two of you in the first place, and then you go and do something like this? Before today, I never would have thought you would try and hurt me this way, but as usual, I was just a little too naive for my own good. And worse than that, you had the audacity to call me this morning like you were so in love with me, like you missed me so much. Hmmph. Isn't that a bitch."

As expected, Larry ignored that last truth and copped out by saying, "This is a terrible situation, I'm confused and right now I don't have the slightest idea about what I want or what I'm going to do."

"So what am I supposed to do while you take the luxury of deciding what you want and who you want it with?"

"I know it might sound cruel, but you're going to have to be patient."

"What about Marilyn? What is she going to have to do?"

"She's going to have to do the same thing."

Regina was hesitant about issuing Larry any kind of an ultimatum right now, but she decided to roll the dice anyway. "Look. With the exception of the last few months, we've had two great years of marriage, and if you want to keep me, you're going to have to get rid of Marilyn as soon as she gets back up here. Not tomorrow, not next week, and not next month. Today."

"Look, Regina, don't push me on this. I told you I'm not sure what I want. I need some time to work things out in my head."

He was starting to sound irritated. What nerve!

"Well, I'll tell you what, as much as it hurts me, I'm not going to accept this shit." Regina heard her voice starting to crack and then elevate. He was pissing her off again. "Men get killed for shit like this every day, and now, more than ever before, I understand what they mean when they say, 'There's a thin line between love and hate,' because as of today, I'm a witness that it sure in the hell is." Regina stood up, walked over to her pile of luggage, picked up her purse and each of the three pieces of baggage she'd brought with her, and headed toward the door, opening it.

Larry stood up. "Where are you going? Do you want me to call down to the front desk and book you another room?"

"Are you going to do the same for Marilyn when she gets back?"

Larry just stared at her with no expression. "I can call down there right now if you want me to."

"You know, you're turning out to be the most inconsiderate, self-centered, sorry-ass man I've ever met. And to answer your question, no, I don't want you to reserve me another room. What you *can* do, though, is kiss my ass. Both you and your black bitch." Regina slammed the door as hard as all of her luggage allowed her to and rested her head against the door. Tears poured down her face so heavily now that she couldn't recognize anything outside her immediate proximity. She had to pull herself together. She wasn't about to stay in the same hotel with her whorish husband or his black-ass mistress. Wasn't even going to stay in the same state with them. She was going to find a restroom, spruce up her makeup, brush through her hair, and book a plane reservation on the first thing smoking back to Chicago.

CHAPTER 9

Aᴏ ᴀʀʀɪᴠɪɴɢ ʜᴏᴍᴇ, Karen took a long, hot, relaxing bubble bath, washed her hair, blow-dried it, and smoothed over it with the curling iron. Although she'd gotten to work late yesterday, she'd still decided to leave at noon today. At first she'd felt guilty about taking time off two days in a row, but since it was already May and she'd hardly taken any vacation time since the end of last year, she didn't see one reason why her boss or anyone else should have a problem with it. Shoot, she'd shown her dedication and then some. And anyway, today was her birthday. She deserved to have at least the afternoon to herself, and she needed ample time to pamper herself and prepare for the big evening out on the town John had promised her. He hadn't given any specifics as far as what they were going to do, but something told her that he was taking her somewhere special.

Maybe even to one of the black production plays down-town. Things were finally getting back to normal with them, and it was about time. He'd kept his word and come straight home with his payroll check last Friday, and when she'd spoken with him at work this morning, he'd assured her he was going to do the same today. All the praying she'd been doing was really working.

Karen sat down on the cream leather sofa in the great room and unscrewed the top of the Harlem Hip Hop nail polish she'd purchased a week ago from her nail techni-cian. Fuchsia was her favorite color, but this had to be the most beautiful shade of it she'd ever seen. Her nails still looked superb from when she'd left the nail salon, but they needed a slight touch-up, since she'd been washing dishes almost every night this week—something John never understood, since their dishwasher was practically brand new.

She stroked the baby finger on her left hand a few times, repeated the same procedure on the other four, and continued onto her right. She'd been getting sculpt-ed acrylic fills for a little over seven years and had been with her current technician, Sharon, for close to five. Sharon was a perfectionist, and Karen admired that about her the most. She was the only technician Karen knew of who, because of sanitary reasons, kept the buffers and files for each of her clients in separate plastic envelopes. She'd always done an excellent job, never a half-ass one like some of those wannabe nail technicians who couldn't care less about customer satisfaction and were only in the business to make a quick buck. Karen had recommended, at minimum, five new customers to Sharon in the last twelve months alone, and each and every one of them swore they had no plans of going anywhere else. The girl was that good.

Karen cautiously picked up the remote control, making sure not to disturb her freshly coated polish, and flicked on the television. There must have been a talk show on every major network channel and even a few of the cable ones. None of the topics looked very interesting to her, so she flipped through the pay channels. Disney, Cinemax, HBO, Showtime, The Movie Channel, and Bravo. They didn't have any decent movies on either. What was the purpose of paying that huge cable bill every month if there wasn't anything on worth watching? But John would literally die if she made the tiniest attempt to cancel the subscription.

She flipped the channel to AMC, the American Movie Classics, and spotted a love story with Cary Grant. It appeared to be one of the few Cary Grant movies she hadn't seen, so she decided to watch. Half of it was already over, but at least it looked like it was interesting enough for her to pass the time until her nails were completely dry.

After an hour elapsed, the movie ended and Karen turned off the television. It was getting close to the time for John to get home from work, so she figured she'd go upstairs and start laying out her clothing. She wondered why she hadn't heard from Regina this morning, since she usually called her every day whenever she was away on a trip. Not to mention, Regina had never missed calling her to wish her a happy birthday for as long as she could remember. But then, she was probably having the time of her life shopping at some boutique and just hadn't found the time yet.

Karen rose from the sofa and heard the doorbell ringing. Who could possibly know she was home this afternoon? She'd purposely not told a soul so that she wouldn't have to be bothered with anyone. If it was some get-rich-quick salesman trying to solicit something, she was going to get rid of him as soon as she opened the door.

The bell rang again. "Just a second."

When Karen pulled the door open, she saw Regina standing there with bloodshot eyes and looking as though someone had just died in her immediate family. What in the world was she doing back here so soon? She'd left not even forty-eight hours ago. "Girl, why'd you come back from Atlanta so quickly?"

Regina burst into tears, with her body trembling uncontrollably, and said nothing.

"What's wrong, Regina?" Karen placed her arms around her friend and escorted her inside. "What happened?"

Karen led Regina to the sofa and hurried to sit her down. It was obvious that Regina was too weak to continue standing and wasn't far from collapsing down on the floor. "Girl, talk to me. Tell me what's wrong?"

By now, Regina was whimpering and sounded like she

was having a difficult time breathing. "Larry . . . and . . . Marilyn . . ."

"Larry and Marilyn what?" Karen was confused.

"I . . . can't ... believe . . . they'd do . . ." Regina muttered and cut the sentence off again.

This girl was acting as though she was having a nervous breakdown, and Karen was scared. "Regina, please try and calm yourself down so you can explain to me what has happened. I can't help you if you don't tell me what's going on," Karen said, picking up the box of Kleenex she'd been using while doing her nails. It was a good thing she hadn't had to go look for it, because Regina was in no kind of shape to be left alone. Not for one minute. Karen snatched out a couple of tissues and passed them to her.

Regina wiped her face, blew her nose, swallowed hard, and took a deep breath. "When I got to Atlanta yesterday, I found Marilyn in Larry's hotel suite stepping out of the shower."

Karen bugged her eyes and dropped her mouth wide open. "You found who?"

"You heard me. Marilyn. She and Larry are messing around, and from the looks of it, it's been going on for some time now."

"How did you catch them? I mean, why did Larry let you in, in the first place, if he knew Marilyn was in his room?"

Regina kicked off her slip-ons, drew her left knee up on the sofa, and turned toward Karen. "First of all, when

I knocked on the door, he opened it and walked away. He thought I was room service bringing up their food. When he realized it was me, though, he had a strange look on his face, but I just figured he was shocked because he had no idea I was coming down there. Then, after I hugged him, I heard the shower shut off, and when I asked him why it had just shut off like that, he said, 'I really wish you had told me you were flying down here.' I knew something wasn't right, so I went into the bathroom and sure enough, Marilyn had her no-good ass stepping out of the shower and was looking as if she had every right to be there."

"Girl, no. Then what?"

"Marilyn started talking a bunch of shit, and I slapped her ass. Larry jumped between us and tried to hold Marilyn, but we started going at it anyway. It was such a nightmare."

"Girl, you don't know what I would have given to have been there with you, so that silly bitch could have gotten a piece of me too. I knew that slut wasn't your friend. She's been jealous of you and Larry the whole time you've been married. And wait a minute. Didn't Marilyn go shopping with you last week when you were buying that lingerie for your trip?"

"Yeah, she knew I was going all the time and never said one word. She wanted me to find out about them, and that's why she didn't say anything."

"Oooh. Just hearing this shit makes me sick to my stomach. What Marilyn needs is her little ass kicked, and

I wouldn't mind being the one who gives it to her. You know I never liked that bitch in the first place."

"I know, and I wish I had listened to you. It's just that she acted like she was such a good friend of mine. I mean, I really liked Marilyn. I can't believe I was so naive."

"What did Mr. Larry say to all of this?"

"Not much. And he had the audacity to say he needed time to think about what he wanted and what he was going to do. Can you believe that shit?" Regina said and started crying again.

"Hell, what does he have to think about? I just know he's not actually considering leaving you for Marilyn, is he?"

"To tell you the truth, I don't know. He sounded so unsure of himself yesterday, and I'm scared to death. I'm pissed off at him and at the same time, I'm hurt. I feel like I'm losing it."

"Girl, I am so sorry."

Regina covered her face.

"When did you get back?" Karen asked.

"Last night about midnight."

"Last night? Why didn't you call me? Girl, you know I've told you a thousand times to call me whenever you need me. No matter what time it is. Especially when something this serious is going on."

"I wanted to call you before I left Atlanta, and again when I made it home, but I just couldn't force myself to talk to anybody. Not even you. I finally took a sleeping pill and cried myself to sleep around six o'clock this morning. I didn't wake up until noon, and when I tried to call you at work, your message said you were gone until Monday. That's when I decided to take a shower, get dressed, and drop by here."

"I still wish you had called me last night. I just told you yesterday before you left that I'm always here for you."

"I almost decided to wait and call you tomorrow morning, because I didn't want to spoil your birthday. And by the way, happy birthday."

"Thanks. And I really appreciate the black balloons you had delivered to my office. You know you didn't have to do that."

"Girl, that's the least I could do. You're the only person I know who still gets excited about birthdays after they've passed twenty-nine. I'm just glad I ordered them two days ago, because with everything that has happened, I probably wouldn't have remembered to do it today."

"So what are you going to do now, and when is Larry supposed to be back in town?"

"Girl, I don't know the answer to either one of those questions. As far as I know, Marilyn stayed down there with him. He even had the nerve to ask me if I wanted him to book me another room to stay in."

"You have got to be kidding me. Is that Negro crazy? Did he actually think you were going to stay at the same hotel in another room while he laid up in his with Marilyn?"

"You know me well, because those were my thoughts exactly."

"I just don't know what to say, Regina, because this has totally caught me off guard. Never in a million years would I have expected something like this from Larry. He's never seemed like the screwing-around type to me. Had he been acting different or anything?"

Regina paused for a minute. "Well, I hadn't told you, because I wasn't sure, but I sort of suspected that he was messing around, because he's been working a ton of overtime, and you know he's been going out every Friday, claiming to play cards. He didn't get home though until after two o'clock on the last two occasions."

Karen just shook her head.

"And girl, Marilyn busted him all the way out. She said that he'd told her to call our house and hang up if I answered, that he'd been at her condo every Friday night for the last few weeks, and that he was with her whenever he was telling me he had to work overtime. Even said that she'd gone on his last two business trips with him."

"What? This is crazy. And if you ask me, both Larry and Marilyn need the shit beat out of them. I mean, how low-down can two people be?"

"I don't know, but I can tell you one thing, Larry and I will never be the same with each other again. I do still love him, and I have no intention of just throwing our marriage away, but it's going to take a long time before I can forgive him for this."

Forgive him? How could Regina even be thinking

about something like that right now? Karen didn't understand any of this, but she was going to keep her mouth shut. She didn't want to hurt Regina's feelings.

"I'm so sorry for dropping in like this on your birthday, but I didn't have anyone else to turn to."

"I'm glad you did come by, and I would have been upset with you if you hadn't."

"What are you and John doing for your birthday?"

"He wouldn't tell me, but I have a feeling it's going to be something nice. As a matter of fact, he should be here any minute."

"I better get out of here so you guys can spend some time together. And I know you both have to get dressed."

"You don't have to leave, and if you want, you can come hang out with us."

"Now, you know there is no way I'm going to ruin whatever John has planned for the two of you," Regina said, standing up.

"Well, like I said earlier, if you need me, I want you to call me. I don't care what time it is. Okay?"

Regina started toward the front door. "I'll be okay, but I'll call you if I need you. If Larry gets back tonight, maybe we can talk things over and put all of this mess into perspective."

"Girl, I wish you the best, and I'll be praying for you," Karen said, hugging Regina.

"You and John have a good time tonight, and call me tomorrow when you get a chance. I'll see you later." Regina moved slowly down the walkway.

"You take care of yourself."

Karen shut the front door and strode over to the staircase. Her heart ached for Regina the same as if it had happened to her. This was unreal. Larry was actually screwing around with Marilyn. No matter how many times she played that thought in her head, she still couldn't believe it. Regina was so in love with this man. One hundred percent faithful to him. What if Larry really left her? She'd completely lose her mind if he did. Karen placed her foot on the bottom stair and thought, "It just goes to show, you never know what might be going on behind closed doors."

WITH THE EXCEPTION OF putting on her close-fitting, black crepe dress, Karen was ready. Her hair was pinned nicely in an up-do, her makeup looked stunning, and she'd just slipped on a black lace bra, matching bikini panties, and jet-black panty hose. It was after six o'clock, and she wondered what was taking John so long. Usually, he punched out around three, and it only took him about an hour to drive home. She'd been trying not to think the worst and figured maybe he was picking her up a last-minute birthday gift, like he usually did every year, but now she was starting to get worried. The last thing she needed was to get into it with him for going to the track on her birthday. But then, he would never have the audacity to do that today. Would he? She was going to give him the benefit of the doubt and wait another half hour before allowing herself to get upset. To move the time along, she picked up the phone and called to check on Regina.

"Hello?" Regina said.

"Hey, I just thought I'd call to see how you were."

"As good as can be expected, I guess."

"Have you heard from Larry since you left here?"

"No. Not one single word. I thought he would have at least called to see how I was, but I guess that's not important to him anymore."

"Maybe he's just trying to let things settle because he knows how upset you are."

"Right now, I'm more hurt than anything else. I've cried so much within the last twenty-four hours that I don't even have any more tears left to shed."

"I can't even imagine what you must be going through, but I'm about to get upset myself. John got off work over three hours ago, and he's still not home."

"You don't think he's out betting on those horses again, do you?"

"At first I didn't, but the only times he hasn't called to let me know he's going to be late coming home is when he's sneaked off to the track. And I'm starting to believe that that's where he is right now. And if he is, girl, this is it. I can't put up with this shit anymore. I had thought maybe he'd taken me more seriously two weeks ago, when I told him he was going to have to get out, but apparently he didn't. I love John more than life itself, but I'll be damned if I'm going to keep living like this. My stomach is always upset, and I never had one problem with my blood pressure until I started all of this worrying about money."

"Girl, you'd better think twice before kicking John out, because I'm telling you from experience, being alone is no fun. I feel so empty that I could just scream. And it's only been one day. It's just not worth it. Screwing around is probably the worst thing a man can do to his wife, and if I'm willing to forgive Larry for that, I know you can forgive John for gambling away some money."

"But that's just it, he's not just gambling some money away, he's getting rid of *all* of it. His whole freakin' paycheck. And just maybe if I put his ass out, he'll know I mean business and that he has no choice but to get some kind of counseling. Or at least start attending those support group meetings like I've been suggesting to him from the very beginning."

"I still think you need to give him another chance. Talk to him one last time and get him to see that you guys can't make it like this. Let him know that your income is the one paying all the bills. Men don't like feeling as though they're being taken care of by a woman, and that will probably change his whole way of thinking. Plus, I know you don't want to hear this, but you did marry him for better or worse."

"I know that, but I'm not putting him out because he has a problem. I'm doing it because he refuses to get help for it. This certainly isn't something he's going to be able to quit on his own."

"Well, I know you have to do what you have to do, but please at least think about it some more. Maybe he's not even at the track in the first place."

"Oh, he's there. Look how long we've been on the phone. The minutes are steadily passing by, and as you can see, he hasn't showed up."

Regina didn't say anything.

"Listen at me. I didn't mean to carry on and on about John. You're the one I'm worried about, and that's the reason I called you."

"Actually, there's not much I can say or do until I talk to Larry. Maybe he'll be back tonight, maybe he won't. Who knows?"

"He'll be back. He can't stay in Atlanta forever."

"Yeah, I guess."

"Well, I better let you go so you can get some rest. I know it's probably hard to go to sleep, but at least you can lie down and rest your nerves," Karen said, slipping off her panty hose.

"Shoot, I don't know if my nerves will ever be at rest, because even if we work things out, I'll always be worried about him messing around, and I don't know if I'll ever be able to trust him again."

"Yeah, I know what you're saying. Well, I'm going to let you go, and I'll check on you first thing tomorrow morning."

"Okay, and good luck with John."

"See ya later," Karen said and hung up the phone.

Damn John for doing this to her. How could the perfect husband become consumed with such a terrible habit? She didn't know what she was going to do without him, and worse than that, had no idea how she was going to make ends meet. But then it was like she'd said before, she could do bad by herself. And she'd rather do that than continue with the way things were. If she was going to struggle to pay the bills on her salary alone, she was going to be the only one living here. Her decision was made.

CHAPTER 10

"**L**OOK, BABY, let's talk about this," John said, sitting down on the side of the bed where Karen was pretending to still be asleep, the same as she always did when she didn't feel like having sex. Except today, she was pretending for an entirely different reason. They'd argued half the night, and she wasn't in the mood for any more of this mess. She'd told him what the deal was and didn't see where there was anything else left to discuss.

"I don't know what's wrong with me," John continued. "I didn't mean to ruin your birthday, and I definitely didn't mean to go to the horse track. You have got to give me another chance."

By now Karen was steaming. She rolled over and stared at him. "Didn't I tell you two weeks ago that if you went out and blew all of your money, you were getting out of here? Didn't I?"

"I know, baby, but damn. Now I realize I have a problem, and I thought about it all last night. I know I can't do this anymore. I won't even play the lottery. I won't do anything that has to do with gambling. I mean it, baby."

Oh shit, here he was in beg mode again. But, unfortunately for him, it wasn't going to work this time. It hadn't been until after ten o'clock last night that he'd finally brought his inconsiderate, sorry, and, once again, broke ass home. Thanks to him, she'd gotten partially dressed for nothing, worried herself half to death, and, worst of all, spent the evening of her thirtieth birthday completely by her lonesome. He'd known all along what the consequences of going on another binge would be. She thought she'd explained them pretty well, and still he'd completely ignored her.

She swung both of her legs from under the cover and hung them over the side of the bed. "Look, John. I can't put up with this shit anymore. I just can't do it. It's a shame that we have to split up over money, but I've given you more than enough chances to stop this craziness. Maybe after we've been apart for a while, you'll take our marriage more seriously, and you might just grow up."

"I told you I'm through with gambling," John said, raising his voice. He was easing out of beg mode and starting to get angry.

Karen stood up and walked over to the dresser. "I just know you're not trying to raise your voice at me. Do you have any idea how much money you've blown over the last couple of months? No, I'm sure you don't. Eight weeks times approximately $850 adds up to sixty-eight hundred. Do you know how much the mortgage payment on this house is? How much the utilities run? How much the notes are on both cars? And let's not forget about credit cards and insurances. I've been taking money from my credit union left and right to make up your gambling losses, and if I'm going to keep having to do that, I'm living here by myself."

"Where the hell am I supposed to go, Karen," John said, rising from the edge of the bed.

"To tell you the truth, I don't care where you go, but I'm sure your mother would love having her thirty-nine-year-old little boy living back at home with her. Our separation will be the best news she's heard all year. She doesn't think you belong with any woman except her, anyway."

John walked toward her. "Look, baby. I'm pleading with you. We can work this out, and if you love me the way you're always saying you do, you'll give me one more chance."

He was looking so pitiful. Sort of like a five-year-old kid who'd just been caught with his hands inside the cookie jar and was sorry for it. As much as she hated to admit it, a part of her wanted to help him. "Okay, I'll tell you what. If you agree to start going to Gamblers Anonymous on a regular basis, we can try and work this thing out."

"I've told you before, I'm not some crazy person,"

John said, throwing both his hands in the air, clearly getting upset again. "I can control this on my own, and you're just going to have to trust me on that."

Damn. If she'd been on the phone with him, she'd have sworn they were having a bad connection. He was acting as if he hadn't heard one word she'd said. The man had thrown away almost seven thousand dollars and still had the nerve to keep insisting that he didn't have a problem. That he didn't need some serious help. Shit. What tiny, little bit of patience she'd had for him one minute ago was gone.

"It's either going to the support group meetings or moving in with your mother. Take your choice," Karen said, brushing her hair and gazing at John through the mirror.

"I can't believe you're actually doing this shit. My name is on the deed to this house the same as yours, so really I don't have to go anywhere. And that's that."

"If you don't, your life with me will become a living hell. And if you keep pushing me, I'll file for a divorce and get rid of your ass for good. Hell, I'm already to the point where I can hardly stand to look at you, and if we stay in this house one more day together, I'll end up hating your guts. So, you see, you really don't have any other alternative except to move out. That's just the way it is."

John stormed out of the bedroom and mumbled what sounded like the word *bitch* under his breath.

"What did you call me," Karen screamed.

John didn't respond, which meant she'd heard him right.

"You worthless son-of-a-bitch," she yelled and slammed the bedroom door.

JOHN HAD DELAYED packing his things all afternoon, but when he'd realized Karen wasn't going to change her mind, he'd finally started loading up the car. He'd taken all of his crisply starched jeans, sweaters, designer sweatshirts, casual shirts, and dress pants, but he obviously wasn't planning on wearing any of his suits, because each of them was still hanging neatly on the rack on what used to be his side of the walk-in closet. Karen had expected him to try and reason with her one last time before driving off, but he hadn't, and a part of her was hurt over it. It had seemed so simple to tell him to get out, but now that it was reality, it didn't feel so good. He'd only been gone a couple of hours, and she was already trying to figure out what she was going to do without him. What if she'd gone too far this time? Her mother had raised her to be independent and to stand her ground when she believed in something, but she'd also taught her that a successful marriage was based on a sizable amount of give-and-take. John was a good husband, and maybe she hadn't taken enough before kicking him out of there. But on the other hand, she'd been pleading with him to stop throwing all of his money away for two whole months, and with the exception of their joint savings accounts at Bank First, the only other security money they had was the money she was saving at her credit union. And if she kept making weekly withdrawals from that account the way she had been, it wasn't going to be long before that was tapped out, too.

She was in a catch-22 situation. Damned if she did, damned if she didn't. If she'd let him stay, he would have continued betting on those horses and she would've had to keep picking up the slack with her savings account. Now that she'd made him get out, she'd still have to keep picking up the slack with her savings account. It didn't seem right, but the scenario had basically remained the same, and the only noticeable change was the fact that now she was all alone.

She lay across the bed with her eyes tightly shut, trying diligently to hold back tears, but it wasn't long before she failed at it. She curled her body into a ball and wept so hard that her stomach shook repeatedly. She hadn't cried like this since the day her grandmother had passed away. How could she have felt so good about telling John to get out and feel so miserable right now? None of this made any sense.

After sleeping for a couple of hours, she woke up at nine o'clock. John had been gone close to four or five hours, and she hadn't heard one word from him. She knew he had every right to not call her, but still, she needed to know that he was all right. Her first thought was to call his mother's house, but talking to that woman would only increase the intense pounding that was already going on inside her head. She hated ingesting any kind of medicine, but she knew she couldn't make it one more minute without popping two Advil.

She walked into the black-and-white bathroom off the master bedroom, reached inside the medicine cabinet for the bottle, turned on the gold-toned faucet, and filled a thin black ceramic cup with cold water. She tilted her head back and swallowed both pills with one large gulp. The bathroom was wallpapered in black and white, the huge tub and double sink were solid black, and the floor was tiled with smooth, snow-white squares. The decorative towels were black and white, the same as the soap dispenser, soap dish, and toothbrush holder. She was proud of the color scheme she'd chosen for their personal bathroom, especially since she'd dreamed of having one designed in black and white for as long as she could possibly remember. And for the first time since they'd moved into this house, she'd be able to keep it orderly and clean, something that had been virtually impossible whenever John had used it. Dirty towels on the floor. Hair clippings from his mustache and beard. None of that was going to be missed.

She gazed at her sorrowful-looking face. Her eyes were red and puffy, the same way Regina's had been yesterday and basically for the same reason: an inconsiderate husband who didn't seem to care about anyone except himself. But then, maybe not hearing from Regina since yesterday was a sign that she and Larry had worked things out. Karen hoped at least somebody was happy.

She wished she hadn't taken that scarf off earlier to brush her hair, because every one of the black strands sticking out from her head was flying in every possible direction. She looked like some schizo woman who'd recently flown the cuckoo's nest and shouldn't have. She looked bad. Pitiful was more like it. She stroked her hair down as best as she could with both hands and turned on the faucet again. She lowered her face into the sink, splashed it with semi-cold water, and patted it gently with the black velour towel. She stared at herself in the mirror again, hoping to see some improvement, but there wasn't any.

She walked back out to the bedroom and stretched across the bed. She didn't have an appetite, she didn't feel like talking to anyone, and she didn't feel like watching any television. She would've turned on the radio, but it was Saturday night and both WGCI and V103 were probably playing those stupid love songs—songs she usually went out of her way to hear but were the last thing she needed to listen to now that John was gone.

Maybe she should put her pride aside and call his mother's house to see if he'd settled in. She picked up the receiver, dialed the first four digits, and dropped it back on the hook. As much as she wanted to, she couldn't. Because if she did, he'd think their separation was some sort of joke. She'd have to wait at least until tomorrow or the next day. Instead, she rolled over on her right side, fluffed the pillow, and prayed for the double dose of Advil to kick in.

CHAPTER 11

REGINA WAS A WRECK and hadn't slept a wink since taking that catnap yesterday afternoon. It was 9 A.M. and a blessing that it was Sunday. She was in no shape to go to work or anywhere else that required her to look presentable.

She dragged her head off the pillow, heard the phone ring, and frowned. She was going to be highly upset if it wasn't Larry on the other end of that phone line. The man hadn't bothered to call at all yesterday, and for all she knew, he was having the time of his life with that slut Marilyn. She leaned over and looked at the beige Caller ID box, where she saw Marilyn's phone number lit across the tiny, rectangular screen. She pressed the palm of her hand over her mouth in total dismay. He'd actually had the audacity to go to Marilyn's condo before coming home and, on top of that, was calling his own wife from there. The phone rang a fourth time. She quickly picked it up so the answering machine wouldn't. "Hello?"

"Regina?"

Who in the hell did he think it would be? She'd been on the phone with him a whole second and already he was sounding stupid. "Yeah, it's me."

"I'm back in town, and I just wanted to let you know that I'm on my way home. We need to sit down and talk."

"Where are you right now?"

"I'm at Ted's. I didn't want to disturb you, so I asked him to pick me up from the airport."

That lying, no-good bastard. He'd actually forgotten about the Caller ID. "If you're at Ted's," Regina screamed, "then why is that bitch's phone number glaring across this Caller ID screen? Huh?"

"Look, Regina," he said, ignoring the fact that he'd just been cracked, "I'll be there in about twenty minutes, and we'll talk then. I don't want to go into anything over the phone."

"Why didn't you call me yesterday? I'm a nervous wreck. Didn't you even care about what was going on with me? I'm the innocent one in this whole messed-up situation. I don't deserve any of this shit."

"I'll talk to you when I get there. Okay?"

"I want to talk about this right now. You've put me off for three days. I left Atlanta on Thursday night, I didn't hear from you all day Friday, not one word from you yesterday, and now *you're* telling me when we're going to talk? *Please.*"

Larry sighed, obviously frustrated. "I'm hanging up now. I'll see you when I get home. We'll talk then and not before."

Regina parted her lips to yell at him again, but she heard the phone click in her ear. He'd actually hung up on her. She dialed Marilyn's number back, but there was no answer. That was quite all right though, because she was going to be the one to have the last laugh when this was over.

S HE HEARD A CAR pull into the driveway and ran over to the window to see if it was him. It was. She saw him unloading his luggage from the trunk of Ted's car. She didn't move.

After entering the house and climbing the staircase, Larry walked into the bedroom and looked straight at Regina with a guilty look on his face. She didn't give him a chance to say anything.

"So what'd you do, have Ted drop that bitch Marilyn off first? Did she stay in Atlanta with you this whole time?"

"Hey. I'm tired, and all I want to do is have a civilized discussion with you," Larry said, sitting down on the chaise over in the corner, as far away from Regina as the size of the room allowed him to be.

"Tired? What do you think I've been doing for the last three nights? Getting my beauty rest? The least you can do is explain to me why you betrayed me the way you did, and what you plan on doing to rectify all of this."

"First of all, it's like I told you down in Atlanta. I never planned for anything like this to happen, it just did. I tried to break it off with her plenty of times, but the more I tried, the deeper things seemed to get. I feel bad, because I never meant to hurt you. I really didn't. You have to believe that."

"How did all this start? And when? If nothing else, you at least owe me an explanation for that. I want the truth. No matter how bad it is."

Larry didn't say anything the first few seconds. "You're right, I do owe you an explanation, and that's why I told you I wanted to come and talk to you. Remember last summer when your aunt from Memphis came to visit your parents and you went to see her, and I was supposed to drive there after my company's golf playday?"

She looked at him in silence.

He took a deep breath. "Well, right after I'd gotten home to change, the doorbell rang and it was Marilyn. She came in and wanted to know if you were here, and I told her you were in Rockford visiting your aunt from out of town. She wanted to use the phone, so I told her to let herself out after she was finished, and then I went upstairs to take a shower. After I had been in the shower for a few minutes, I saw her opening the shower door. She'd taken all of her clothes off and was just standing there. The next thing I knew, she'd stepped in the shower, and one thing led to another."

"I can't believe you're telling me this," Regina said, forcefully holding back the tears. "Not in my own house, Larry. Please don't tell me that that's where you first had sex with her."

"You said you wanted me to tell you the truth, and that's what I'm trying to do. I'm not enjoying this any more than you are."

"How could you do this to me? Is it that you don't love me anymore? What is it?"

"I do still love you. Not once have I lied to you about that. But as much as I hate to admit it, I'm in love with Marilyn, too."

There. He'd finally said it. He was in love with Marilyn, and there was nothing she could really do about it. Her body was overflowing with pain, and she felt faint. She made her way to the bed and sat down on it. She didn't know what to say to any of this. Never in her wildest dreams had she ever imagined that one day the walls would come crashing down around her like this. How could she ever trust him again? And with the exception of Karen, she'd never trust another woman as long as her heart continued pumping blood through her veins. She was finally crying. Softly, but with obvious emotional pain.

"I'm sorry, baby," he said. "I wish I could change the way things are, but I can't."

"Well, what do you plan on doing now? Have you broken things off with Marilyn?"

"No, I haven't. But I do think it would be best if I moved out of here for a while so that we can all think things through. I've already cleared it with Ted, and he says I can stay with him for a while. I'll still pay the bills, so you don't have to worry about anything like that."

"Bills?" That was the least of her worries at this point. "Larry, it's not going to help us any if you move out. We need to spend as much time together as we possibly can. I know you've made a lot of mistakes, but I'm willing to try and forgive you. I know it will take time, but please don't just throw our marriage away like this. You say that you love me, and you know I love you. We've built too much together to let it all go."

"I'm too confused to stay here. I don't know what I want, and it's not fair for you to have to deal with this. I just think it's best that I move out. At least on a temporary basis. I mean, I'm not saying I don't ever want to be with you again, or that I want a divorce. I'm just saying that we need some time apart."

"Why? I mean, until this Marilyn thing started, we were doing just fine. All you have to do is tell her that it's over between the two of you."

"Regina, the only reason we weren't having any problems was that I never complained about anything you said or did. I always went along with the program just to keep peace between us."

"What are you talking about?"

"I don't want to get you any more upset than you already are, so I'll just leave it at that," he said, walking into the closet. He grabbed a group of pants off the rack and laid them across the chaise.

"Tell me," she said and stood up.

"It's not worth it. It's best to just leave it alone."

"I want to know what you mean when you say you

just went along with the program. Tell me," she said again, louder than before.

"Fine. If you want to know, I'll tell you. I've always despised the fact that you spend every dime you get on a bunch of unnecessary shit and then complain about how we aren't saving any money. Or how we have so many damn bills to pay. Just look at all this crap you've got in this closet," he said, pointing at her clothing. "Half of it you don't even wear, and still you keep buying more. I'm sick of paying all of the bills and watching you blow your money and any of mine that's left over on material shit. I'm sick of all those credit card bills coming in here. That's not how I want to live the rest of my life. And I'm sick and tired of you breaking your neck to get something just because Karen has it. That's just plain crazy. And most of all, I'm sick of you running around all the time thinking you're Miss It, simply because the shade of your skin is a little lighter than the next person's. The whole time I've known you, you've been color-struck. Hell, I'm light-skinned, too, but I sure as hell don't think I'm better than any dark-skinned brother, and I'd be stupid if I did."

She was stunned. She'd had no idea he was this miserable with her. That he'd had all of these complaints and dislikes. If she'd had any feelings left, she'd be hurt. Was she that terrible with money? And she knew he wasn't serious when he said she was color-struck. She never disliked people or treated them any differently simply because they were dark-skinned. She simply thought that light-skinned people were more attractive. But she didn't think she was better in general. And the only reason she and Karen ended up with so many of the same things was that they had the same taste. It had been that way since they were children. "I don't know what you're talking about," she finally said.

"No, I didn't think you would. But I know you're not going to stand there and pretend nobody has ever said anything to you about blowing money or making those comments about color all the time, like you do. I know better than that."

"No, as a matter of fact, not one person has ever said anything about me being color-struck. And if I spend too much money, all you had to do was tell me about it. Not go out and start screwing some bitch like Marilyn."

"Weren't you just listening to me? It's not just that, it's your whole attitude," he said, bunching together some of his dress socks from the dresser drawer.

"Why don't you just admit it," she said, walking toward him. "It's not my attitude, it's that ugly, black bitch you've been messing around with that's causing you to act like this."

"You see, that's the kind of shit I'm talking about. You know just as well as I do that Marilyn is far from being ugly, and the only reason you're saying that is because she's dark. It's just too much for you to accept that she looks just as good as you do."

"Why are you talking to me like this? You come in here saying you're sorry and how you didn't mean to hurt me, and now you're talking to me this way? What's the matter with you? It's like you're up one minute and down the next. Just because you've gone out there and made an ass of yourself doesn't mean you have the right to treat me like this."

"Look. I'm not arguing with you about this anymore. I thought I could come over here and have an adult conversation, but the only thing this is turning into is a screaming match."

"Why are you going to stay with Ted, when you can stay right here? This house is certainly big enough for both of us. We don't even have to sleep in the same bedroom if you don't want to. I'm telling you, if you walk out that door, things will never be the same between us again. Maybe we just need to see a marriage counselor, since you say I'm doing so many things you don't like. Let's at least try that."

"My mind is made up. I thought about it a lot over the last couple of days, and this is the best way to do this. If I stay here, all we're going to do is argue."

"Are you going to see Marilyn while we're separated?"

"I don't know what I'm going to do. I'm moving out because I need to clear my head, not find a convenient way to see her."

Quite obviously. Almost every day of the week had been convenient until she'd busted him three days ago. "Please, Larry. Don't leave like this. At least give our marriage a chance." The sound of her own voice sickened her. He'd been screwing around on her for almost a year, and here she was begging him not to leave her.

He ignored what she'd just said and continued gathering his underwear and ties together. He'd just finished packing his colognes and other toiletries in the overnight bag when Regina went to the bed and started pulling out the items he'd already packed. "I won't let you leave like this. If you stay here, we can work on keeping our marriage together. Just give it a week, and then if you still feel the same, I won't stand in your way. I promise."

"Don't take anything else out of that suitcase," he said with anger flowing through his voice. "I mean it, Regina. I'm not playing with you."

Dear God. This wasn't the same Larry she'd married two years ago. Not even a slight resemblance, for that matter. What was wrong with him? Why was he so irate and disrespecting her the way he was? She was almost afraid to say anything else, but before she knew it, the words were already passing through her lips. "Why are you so angry? Why are you treating me like this?"

"Because. I told you I was sorry. I told you the truth about Marilyn, and now you're harassing me about leaving. I told you my mind was made up, and still, you keep hounding me about it. The last thing I wanted was for us to end up at each other's throats like this."

"Okay. Fine. I'll leave you alone. But the only reason I'm trying to stop you from leaving is because I love you more than anything in this world, and I don't want to lose you. I thought that meant something to you." She was crying again.

"It does mean something, and I love you too, but it's still best that we separate for a while," he said, zipping up the garment bag and throwing it across his arm. He picked up the smaller suitcase and overnight bag. "I'll be back sometime this week to get some more of my things. Maybe I'll see you then, okay?"

She walked back over to the window and stared down to the street. She wasn't about to watch him walk out that door. "Whatever, Larry," she said quietly.

"I'm sorry for all of this, and I wish there was some way I could make it up to you." He walked through the doorway, down the stairs, and into the garage to load the Lexus.

She couldn't stand to see him back out of the driveway, so she moved away from the upstairs window. When she heard the garage door closing, she knew he was gone. She leaned against the wall. "Oh God, please help me. How could he do something like this?" She wailed loudly, dropped to the floor, and curled up like a frightened child. She was better off dead. She couldn't live her life without Larry. Everything inside her depended on him. How was she going to make it through another day knowing that he was in love with another woman? Someone who had claimed to be her friend. Someone she had trusted. Her perfect marriage had transformed itself into a horrible nightmare and didn't appear to have any chance of a happy ending. She needed one of those sleeping pills she'd been taking. No, what she needed were as many as were left in the bottle. What reason could she possibly have for waking up again anyway? Clearly, there wasn't one she could think of.

CHAPTER 12

"I SHOULD BE THERE in about fifteen minutes," Karen said.

"I'll be watching out for you," Regina said, brushing over her red hot fingernail polish with Sally Hansen's top coat. She was sitting on the sofa in the family room.

Regina wasn't in the mood for going to church, but since it was Mother's Day, she figured the least she could do was attend services with her parents. And it would probably do her some good, since she'd had those crazy, suicidal thoughts just one week ago. She couldn't believe she'd even toyed with the idea of doing something so idiotic. No man was worth taking her life over, no matter what the circumstance, and she was glad she'd realized that before it had been too late.

She walked into the living room, sat down on the off-white wingback chair in front of the window, and crossed her legs. She glanced down at her evergreen shoulder bag and realized she hadn't switched purses. She'd planned on pulling out her red one with the chain shoulder strap, but she had completely forgotten about it. She preferred complete color coordination whenever she wore her Sunday-go-to-meeting suits because those were a lot dressier than the ones she wore to work.

She was decked out in a bright red, tailored-looking linen suit and a pair of elegantly sculptured red pumps. This evergreen purse wasn't going to do. She'd have Karen make the change for her as soon as she arrived, so she wouldn't ruin her manicure.

She leaned back in the chair to relax, and something dawned on her. She hadn't thought about Larry for almost ten minutes. She'd thought her loneliness would become easier to deal with as the days went on, but it hadn't. He hadn't called her, and the few times she'd called him at work he'd said he was too busy to talk. She took a deep breath. She felt like crying again, and it took all of the willpower she had to prevent it. Was this ever going to get any better? Was he ever coming back to her? And how were her parents going to take all of this? At this point, she hadn't told them about how their loving son-in-law had walked out on their only child. She'd have no choice but to tell them today though, because her mother would take one look at her and know that something was gravely wrong.

* * *

BEHIND CLOSED DOORS

FTER KAREN switched Regina's wallet, lipstick, facial powder, and a few other personal items into her red purse, they left and started on their way to Rockford. Generally, it took about an hour, but whenever Karen drove, they usually got there in record time. The girl had a lead foot that just wouldn't quit.

As they arrived at the Elgin toll center, Karen tossed forty cents into the basket, waited for the wooden slat to lift, pressed on the accelerator, and steered the Jeep out of the stall. She was sharper than a piece of broken glass and knew it. She was dressed in an off-white acetate rayon suit, an off-white pair of panty hose, and an off-white pair of mules. She'd accented the outfit with pearl earrings and a larger pearl necklace.

Karen always liked listening to Pam, the DJ for V103's Sunday morning gospel show, but she turned down the volume on the radio, so she and Regina could talk. "So, Larry still hasn't called yet?"

"No," Regina said, positioning her bottom on the passenger seat. "I've called him at work, but he claims he's too busy to talk. I called Ted's house a couple of times, but Ted said he wasn't there. He was probably with that—" She wanted to call Marilyn a bitch, but she figured that was an inappropriate word to be using since they were on their way to church. "Well, you know who I'm talking about."

"You think? Maybe he's not. Maybe he just needs some time to himself."

"Now, Karen. You know just as well as I do that he's

still seeing her. If he was doing it before we separated, what's to stop him now?"

"Yeah, I guess you're right about that. Did he say why he did what he did? I mean, I know you told me he was unhappy with a lot of things, but you never gave me any specifics. Which I'm still mad about, since you didn't call me right when he left. I would've come right over, and you know it. This is the second time you've needed me and haven't called to let me know it."

The reason Regina hadn't called was that she'd been contemplating killing herself. But there was no need to elaborate on that now. "Well, for one thing, he said I spend too much money. And I admit that sometimes I spend a lot of unnecessary money on things I don't need, but I don't see why he's just now letting me know how he feels about it. He had mentioned it a couple of times before, but he'd never made a big deal out of it."

"Please. That still doesn't justify him going out and committing adultery," Karen said, rolling her eyes upward in disgust.

"Yeah, I know it's not, but tell him that. Oh yeah, and he also said that I'm color-struck, and that I think I look better than dark-skinned women. Which really upset me, because I don't think I'm better than anybody."

Karen didn't say anything.

"Have you ever thought that about me?"

"Thought what?" Karen asked evasively.

"Do you think I'm color-struck? Just be honest."

Karen didn't like this at all, because it was obvious that

Regina really didn't understand what Larry was talking about. "Look. You're my best friend, and we all have faults. I know I do. I'm probably one of the most opinionated, stubborn people you'll ever meet. Not to mention the fact that I like to have my way with a lot of things."

"We're not talking about you, though. What I want to know is if you think I'm color-struck."

"I probably wouldn't go as far as saying that, but you do make a lot of comments when it comes to color. That's just the way you are, and I'm used to it. It doesn't mean you're a terrible person or anything," Karen said, staring straight ahead of her. She couldn't look Regina in the face now if she wanted to.

"Comments like what?" Regina asked, turning toward Karen.

"Well, for example, whenever you describe how a guy looks, you always have to say whether he was light or whether he was dark. Most of the time you don't even say 'light-skinned,' you say 'bright-skinned.' Do you remember a couple of months ago when we were at that cafe down in the Loop, and that real nice-looking guy passed by and smiled at you?"

"Yeah, I think so."

"Do you remember what you said?"

"No. What?"

" 'He sure was dark, but he was fine, though.' "

"But I didn't mean anything by it."

"Yeah, but when you say it like that, it's like you're

saying it's a rarity for a dark-skinned person to look good."

"That's not what I meant at all," Regina said, sounding defensive.

"Okay," Karen said. "What about the time you were telling me about how beautiful your cousin's kids were that live in St. Louis? You said, 'Tamara's kids are so gorgeous. All three of them are so bright-skinned.'"

"What's wrong with describing how they look?"

"Nothing, except that whenever you say a light-skinned person looks good you make it sound as though that's why they look good, and whenever you say a dark-skinned person looks good, you make it sound like it's so unusual."

"How come you've never mentioned this before?"

"That's just the way you are, and when you've been friends with someone for as long as I've been with you, you accept that person, regardless."

"You're dark-skinned, and I don't think I'm better than you." Regina paused. "I don't even let anything like that cross my mind. I think we're both attractive, and I've never seen any reason to make any comparisons between us."

"Well, I never said anything before, but it always seemed like to me that whenever a guy paid more attention to me than to you, you seemed offended. Almost like you couldn't understand why they hadn't chosen to talk to you instead. You never said anything, but you always seemed disappointed. And one time, you even went as far as saying that you knew you weren't ugly, so you couldn't understand why it was so hard for you to meet decent guys whenever we went out."

"That was just a statement. I was only trying to figure out why I wasn't meeting any decent men. That's all."

"Well, maybe you don't mean anything when you say the things you say, but those sort of comments tend to make people think funny. Especially dark-skinned people," Karen said, driving away from the Marengo-Hampshire tollbooth.

Regina rotated her body back toward the front of the car and was silent.

"You shouldn't let any of this bother you, though, because I'll love you like my sister until the day I die. The only reason I told you any of this is because you asked me to. Otherwise, I would have never said anything about it."

"Well, I guess I need to watch what I say, and how I say it, because I certainly don't want to insult anybody simply because they have a certain skin color."

"If I were you, I wouldn't worry about it. You're a good person with a good heart, and that's more important than anything I can think of. And as far as I can tell, you're the same Regina you were when Larry married you. It's not like you've drastically changed your personality all of a sudden. And even if you had, it still doesn't give him the right to go out and see if the grass is greener on the other side. It just doesn't. So, before you start blaming yourself, just remember, you're the victim here. If Larry was unhappy with the way your marriage was going, he should have let you know. Although, I must admit, communication doesn't work for everyone."

"Why do you say that?" Regina asked, stroking the sides of her neatly tapered hair.

"Because when John first started this horse track thing, I tried to talk to him about it, and it didn't work. After a few weeks passed by, I argued with him about it. Then finally, our arguments turned into angry debates, and it wasn't long before I was telling him to get out. And as you can see, that's exactly what he did."

"Have you spoken with him this weekend?"

"The man calls every day. Calls me at work and at home, begging me to let him come back."

"Girl, you must be out of your mind," Regina said, moving her head from side to side. "Larry has gone out and screwed another woman, but if he called me tonight, saying he wanted to come back home, I'd welcome him back with open arms. I know it might sound stupid, but like I told you before, I still love him, and I just can't see myself going through life without him."

"Well, I'm not like that. I love John more than anything, and you know I don't want anyone else, but I just can't put up with his gambling. And I know if I hold out long enough, he'll eventually come around and start going to those support meetings."

"But what if he doesn't? Then what are you going to do?"

"I don't know, and to tell you the honest truth, I don't even think like that. I'm not planning to divorce him or anything, I just want him to change what he's doing before we lose everything we've got."

"Life is so strange. When we were six, we were in the same first-grade class. When we were twelve, we got our periods for the first time. When we were seventeen, we graduated high school a whole year early and then enrolled at the same university. By the time we were twenty-eight, we had both purchased beautiful homes in the same Chicago suburb. But look at us now, since we turned thirty. We're separated from our husbands and have no idea as to how things are going to turn out. Although, your situation is a little different than mine. Larry left on his own, and there's nothing I can do about it, but all you have to do is say the word, and John would be back today. Shoot, you'd better take my advice and call him. Better yet, you'd better stop by his mother's while we're in Rockford and talk to him personally."

"As bad as I want to see him, and as much as I miss him, I just can't do that. And you know I wouldn't dare step foot in his mother's house, anyway."

"Did you hear yourself earlier, saying how stubborn you were? Girl, you'd better put that little pride of yours aside and tell your man he can come home. I've told you that before."

"I'm doing no such thing. You just wait and see. This is the only way to handle John. The man doesn't understand the nicey nicey way with anything and has to learn all his lessons from the School of Hard Knocks."

"Girl, please," Regina said, laughing for the first time

since they'd started their journey. "I don't see how you can joke about this. But then, you always were the strong one. I wish I could be like that, but it's just not in me."

"It's not that I don't get lonely or that I never feel hurt, because I do. But the world doesn't stop simply because things aren't going the way you want them to, so you have no choice except to roll with the punches as they come," Karen commented and glanced at the sign to the right that said, Rockford 36 miles.

"I guess. But that still wouldn't change the fact that I want Larry back. And as far as I'm concerned, nothing else really matters," Regina said, staring out the window.

"Don't worry," Karen said. "Things will work out between the two of you in due time." Karen hoped there was some truth to what she'd just said.

KAREN PULLED INTO her mother's steep, perfectly cemented driveway and parked behind Sheila's Toyota. She hadn't spoken with her sister since that day they'd had those words about Terrance, and she wondered if it had all blown over. She'd practically forgotten about it, but one never could tell what the situation was going to be with Miss Sheila. The girl could hold grudges longer than anybody else Karen knew. She hoped Sheila had gotten over it by now, though, because it didn't make sense to have something that petty spoil the whole day. Mother's Day was supposed to be a happy occasion.

She stepped out of the Jeep, removed the corsages

she'd picked up at the florist after dropping Regina at her parents', and shut the door. She walked up the stairs, onto the porch and inside the house, since the door was already open. Although, she would have done the same even if it had been locked, since she still had her original set of keys from when she was living here. After she'd gone away to college and ultimately moved to Schaumburg, her mother hadn't made her give them up, and she was glad, because regardless of where she lived, she still considered this home.

"Hey," Karen yelled like she always did whenever she entered her mother's house.

She heard three adult voices saying "Hello" from the kitchen—her mother's, Sheila's, and her mother's significant other, Richard's. Before she could set the box of corsages on the dining room table, she saw her niece and two nephews racing toward her and screaming, "Auntie Karen," like they hadn't seen her in ages. She was glad to see them too and hugged each of them one by one, praying that all of their hands were clean, because Lord knows, children and the color white didn't mix.

"How are my little sweethearts doing?" she asked, smiling.

"Fine," they all answered in unison.

"You guys look so cute in your little outfits. I should've brought my camera so I could have taken your picture."

"Granny took us shopping yesterday and bought them for us," Shaniqua quickly offered as important information.

It figured, Karen thought. Sheila was probably too

busy buying that no-good father of theirs something to wear and had no money left from her latest welfare check to buy the kids anything. What a shame. "That was nice of Granny, wasn't it?"

They all shook their heads and mumbled uh-huh.

"Auntie Karen," Shaniqua said. "Jason got in trouble at school again this week, and he got kicked out for five whole days."

"Jason, what did you do?" Karen asked, placing her palm on the top of his head.

He didn't say anything, and that told her it must be pretty bad.

"He told the teacher he wanted to . . . you know, that word that starts with an F that you're always telling William not to use. Anyway, that's what he said he wanted to do to her," Shaniqua said.

"Jason," Karen said, elevating her voice. "You know better than that. You should be ashamed of yourself."

Jason tucked his head, which meant the boy had at least some remorse for his actions, and which also meant that the right discipline would alleviate a great deal of this horrendous behavior of his. But then, it would take a certain kind of mother to give him that, and the poor little thing was far from having one of those.

Karen went into the kitchen and hugged everybody. "You all are looking mighty sharp today."

They all laughed.

"You're looking good yourself with all of that white on," Lucinda complimented back.

"Thanks, Mom."

"You really do look nice in that outfit, Karen," Sheila said, smiling.

"Thanks," Karen said. The verdict was in: Sheila wasn't upset with her anymore.

"Are you guys about ready to get going?" Karen asked.

"Service doesn't start until eleven, but we'd better get started so we can get some halfway decent seats," Lucinda said. "Even the people who don't go to church at any other time of the year seem to find their way to the sanctuary on Easter and Mother's Day. The last couple of years, the balcony was completely filled up, the ushers had to place folding chairs down each of the aisles, and some of the congregation had to squeeze into the choir stand. I don't want to take any chance with us having to do anything like that."

They all gathered into the living room, where Karen pinned a white corsage on Lucinda, since Lucinda's mother was deceased, and a red one on herself. She hadn't bothered to buy one for Sheila or the kids, since she and Sheila hadn't been talking. How was she supposed to know whether they were planning on going to church or not? And of course, Sheila hadn't bothered to buy any either. But, it was too late to be stopping by any flower shop. By now, most of the places were probably sold out anyway.

Karen, Lucinda, Richard, and Shaniqua sat down inside the Jeep, and Jason, William, and Sheila got in her car. Karen turned the key in the ignition, looked back, and saw John blocking the driveway with the Beamer. Oh, no. She was hardly ready to talk to him, and seeing him was only going to make things harder. The fact that he might pull something like this had crossed her mind when she was getting dressed this morning, since she'd told him she was going to church with her mother, but she'd forgotten all about it.

Lucinda looked around, when she noticed Karen gazing through the back window. She smiled when she saw John waving at her. She waved back. "Girl, get on out of here and go talk to that man. You know that's what he's waiting on," Lucinda said, laughing.

Karen rolled her eyes at her mother playfully. This was right up Lucinda's alley, since she'd never accepted the fact that they'd split up in the first place.

"What do you want?" Karen asked as she walked down to the street.

"I want you, with your fine self," John said, grinning.

She almost grinned back, but her grandmother had taught her long ago that it was a grave mistake to show all thirty-twos if a woman wanted a man to take her seriously. "We've got to get out of here, so will you please move this thing?"

"I'll move it if you promise to call me when you get back from taking your mother to dinner."

"How do you know I'm taking Mom out to dinner?"

"Because you always do every year. And anyway, she told me you were, when I called to wish her a happy

Mother's Day this morning. Even said I could go with you guys if I wanted. Maybe that's what I ought to do, too."

It was so fitting that her mother would tell John something like that. Knowing Lucinda, she'd probably coerced John into coming over there, trying to be some matchmaker. "Look, if it will get you to move this car out of my way, I'll call you when I get back. Okay?"

"I miss you, baby."

Shoot, she missed him, too, but she wasn't going to let him know it. "I'll call you when I get back," Karen said, tipping back up the driveway in her heels.

She slid back into the Jeep and shut the car door. She figured the least she could do was talk to him. She wasn't ready to let him move back in yet, like Regina had suggested, but maybe she would start spending a little time with him. It seemed stupid to date her own husband, but that's as far as she was willing to let it go. At least for now.

John drove off, Karen did the same, and Sheila followed behind her in the direction of the church.

CHAPTER 13

"I CALLED THAT BASTARD at least ten times today, and he never even bothered to call me back," Regina said to Karen. They were on their way to their toning session at the health club. Usually they drove separately, but since they were both feeling a bit on the lonely side, they figured they'd might as well ride together and get a bite to eat somewhere afterward. The way they used to do, when it was just the two of them and they didn't have husbands.

"Girl, I don't know what's the matter with Larry. He's really showing his ass," Karen said, adjusting her Anne Klein sunglasses.

"I even tried calling him again at Ted's this morning before I got dressed for work, but like every other time I've called, Ted said he wasn't there. I'll bet you anything he's not staying with Ted. I'll bet he moved in with that slut."

"You think he would do something like that?"

"Hell, yeah. Look at how he's acting toward me. Look how he keeps dodging my phone calls. I'm telling you, this shit is starting to piss me off, and my love for him is slowly turning to hate. I wish I could shoot his no-good ass."

"Girl, don't even think like that. He's not even worth it."

"You know I would never go that far. I'm just saying what I feel like doing." Regina raised her left arm to see what time it was. "Larry should be off work by now. I'm driving by Marilyn's condo to see if his car is parked outside," Regina said, already heading in that direction.

Karen wasn't sure if she liked this or not. She couldn't believe how bold Regina had gotten. It was amazing how being hurt could change so quickly into anger. Usually, Karen would be all for something like this, but Regina was way too upset to be driving by anywhere, let alone where her husband was probably shacking up with some whore. There was no telling what might happen. She had to try and talk Regina out of this. "I wouldn't give him the satisfaction of knowing that you even care where he is or what he's doing."

"No, I'm sick of begging his yellow ass, and I'm sick of all these sleepless nights. You don't know how hard it is for me to get up, get dressed, and struggle through eight hours of work. Shit, I haven't had any decent sleep for almost two weeks, and I've hardly eaten two full meals in the last seven days. And yesterday, when I broke the news to my parents, you would have thought somebody had died. Ma cried through almost all the church service, and Daddy hardly said more than two words the whole time we were at the restaurant. Instead of them supporting me, I spent the rest of Mother's Day trying to console the two of them. I thought about this shit all last night and most of today, and I'm sick of taking this off of Larry. If he won't talk to me on the phone, I'll make his sorry ass do it in person."

Karen had known all along that Regina was planning to do more than just drive by there. She could hear it in her voice from the beginning. Usually, Karen was the one with the don't-take-no-shit attitude, but Regina was acting rather courageous today. For the first time in a long time, Regina scared her, and Karen hoped Larry still had his ass at work.

Regina slowed the Mercedes and stopped directly across the street from Marilyn's brick condominium. As expected, Larry's Lexus was parked right in front. Regina squinted her eyes in anger, and without even realizing it, threw her car in park, jumped out, slammed the door, and stormed up the sidewalk. She rang the doorbell over and over again, like most children do when they don't know any better.

"Regina," Karen yelled while leaning out the car window.

"All I'm going to do is talk to him. Nothing more," Regina yelled, turning back toward the door. She continued to bang on it and rang the doorbell repeatedly.

No one answered.

They were trying Regina's patience. "I know you've got your silly ass up in there, Larry, so you might as well bring it on out here right now."

The noise must have been carrying all the way across the street, because Regina saw Karen step outside the car and walk around to the back of it. She must've been positioning herself just in case she had to intervene.

Regina glanced over at the window to the right of the front door and saw Marilyn peek out at her and then close the blind in a hurry. Regina laughed. "Well, isn't that a bitch. You were acting like the Wicked Witch of the Midwest, when we were down in Atlanta. Like you were some bold bitch. But look at your coward ass now." Regina was loving every bit of this because it was obvious that Marilyn was terrified that maybe she and Karen had shown up to kick her home-wrecking ass.

"Open up this got-damn door, bitch," Regina continued. "I'm not leaving until you send my husband out here. You can come too, if you want to. You're just like part of the family now, anyway."

Still, nothing.

Regina was fed up. She was sick of being ignored, and she was going to get their attention one way or the other. She walked out to the curb, searching up and down it, then grabbed a medium-sized rock.

"Girl, are you crazy?" Karen asked, walking toward her. "Let's go. He's not worth this, and you know it. What if they call the police on your butt?"

"Uh-uh, he's trying to play me for some kind of a fool, and I'm not putting up with this shit anymore," Regina said, moving into target range of the Lexus.

Larry, who'd clearly been watching her every move, swung open the front door when he saw her pull her arm back, preparing to hurl the rock through his car window.

"What's the matter with you?" he yelled, running across the lawn and down to where Regina was standing.

"There's nothing the matter with me. What the hell is the matter with your lying ass?" Regina asked, lowering her fist back down to her side.

"This is not the time or the place for us to discuss our personal business. Let's just meet somewhere and talk about this like two adults. Okay?"

"Oh, now you want to act like two adults, huh? Well, too damned bad, because that's what I've been trying to do for the last ten days. You didn't pay me any attention, though, did you? So, I figured I'd lower myself to your level and start acting like a child. I've been calling you every day, and you've been acting like it's no big deal. Like you couldn't care less. And I know you didn't fix your lips to say 'Let's meet somewhere.' You must be out of your mind. Why would I meet you somewhere when we have a home over in Wesleyan Estates? Remember? Or have you suddenly forgotten about that?"

"Regina, come on and get in the car," Karen said. Now Larry was starting to piss her off, too, but she didn't want to say anything she might regret. Especially since their situation wasn't any of her business in the first place.

Regina ignored her. "So, tell me, Larry, are you still staying with Ted?"

"I'm not going to discuss anything standing out here on the street. I can't believe you're embarrassing me like this and making such a fool of yourself."

Regina looked around the neighborhood and saw four or five people acting as though they had important business on their front lawns, but it was obvious that they were more concerned with the commotion she and Larry were creating. But what did she care? She didn't have to live in this neighborhood. "You should've thought about that before you started sticking your dick between Marilyn's legs."

"You are impossible," Larry said, walking back up to the condominium. "I'll talk to you when you're in a more civilized state. Right now, though, I can't deal with you."

"Don't walk away from me, Larry. I'm telling you, if you know what's good for you, you won't do it."

He waved his hand at her and continued up to the front door without looking back.

"You doggish motherfucker," Regina screamed and tossed the rock as hard as she could at the window on the driver's side of the Lexus.

Larry turned around when he heard the crash, and saw the ruptured glass shattering piece by piece onto the pavement. He rushed back out to the street. "What did you do that shit for? You are one silly bitch."

"No, you're the bitch. You weren't even man enough

to tell me you wanted someone else, and you're still not man enough to face me now."

"You'd better stop pushing me, Regina, before I have you arrested. I'm not playing with you."

"And who are you? Because I'll say and do whatever I damn well please, brother," Regina said, moving closer to him. "And what police officer do you know of that will arrest me for damaging my own car? I might not ever drive your precious little car, but my name is on the title as big as day."

"I told you, you'd better stop pushing me. Karen, you'd better get your friend before I hurt her."

Wait a minute. Karen just knew he wasn't talking to her. And she hoped, for his sake, he wasn't thinking about hitting Regina. That shit wasn't going to work. "Regina, let's go, okay, before this mess gets out of hand," Karen finally said. "You can deal with this later."

"No, I'm not going anywhere," Regina said, jumping in Larry's face. "What do you mean, before you hurt me? I wish you would. I'll have your ass locked up so fast, you'll wish you'd never even thought about touching me."

Damn. Karen wished Regina would stop this, because it was obvious that Larry was running out of patience and was becoming more and more annoyed. She'd known from the very beginning that it was a serious mistake for Regina to come over here, and she could kick herself for not stopping her.

Larry pushed Regina away from him, causing her to

stumble. "I'm telling you one more time. You'd better get the hell away from me."

"Regina, let's go," Karen said, raising her voice this time.

"You'd better listen to your friend before I do more than push your silly ass," Larry said, gazing at the broken glass again and shaking his head.

"Just try it, Larry. You're just mad because I came over here and interrupted your little program. And I'm telling you now, this is only the beginning. I've shed tear after tear and lost I don't know how many hours of sleep, but I'm through crying and now you're the one who's about to have the sleepless nights. I promise you that."

Regina glanced over at Marilyn, who was now bravely standing inside the doorway like nothing had happened. She hadn't said one word the whole time. Didn't seem one bit disturbed by what she'd just seen. But, then, why should she? She had exactly what she wanted: someone else's husband giving her sex, probably money, and the relationship she'd always craved. What a ruthless bitch. "What the hell are you staring at? I should come up there and whip your little two-faced ass."

Karen politely walked over to Regina, who was still yelling and screaming, grabbed her by the arm, and pulled her toward the car.

"I'm getting your rotten ass for this, Larry. Just watch. Every dog has his day, and you'd better believe the day is coming for you and your black bitch," Regina shrieked, being dragged across the street against her will.

"No, your day is the one coming," he said furiously.

"Much sooner than you think. You're about to get the surprise of your life, and I can't wait for it to happen."

"And what is that supposed to mean? You planning to divorce me?"

"Girl, get your butt in the car," Karen said, leading Regina to the passenger seat. She shut the door, walked over to the driver's side, turned on the ignition, and snapped the seat belt at her waist. Her legs were much longer than Regina's, so she had to adjust the side mirrors and the seat.

Regina barely closed the door before Karen started down the street.

"Can you believe that shit?" Regina asked Karen. "I can't believe he actually pushed me like that."

"To tell you the truth, I can't either, but then, I can't believe anything he's been doing to you lately. He's clownin'."

"I don't know whether I'm hurt or mad or what. I guess I'm both. But I do know one thing, I'm tired of begging him. Pleading with him like he's some king or something. I decided today that I can't go on like this anymore. I do want to work things out with him, but I'm starting to realize he's not interested in trying to make that happen. He's acting like Marilyn's got him pussy-whipped. I could just strangle her simpleminded, conniving ass. Oooh."

"Yeah, I was thinking the same thing when I saw how he was acting toward you. It's almost like she's voodood him or something," Karen said, rolling the window down a little further so she could get a bit more fresh air. "I mean, he's acting like she's got complete control over his attitude, his emotions, and although I hate to agree with you, his dick."

Regina laid her elbow just below the bottom of the window and rested her head in her hand. All of a sudden she felt like crying. Her emotions were so volatile these days, as they were each month when she got PMS, right before her little red wagon rode in. "Sometimes I feel like this is a bad dream that I can't wake up from."

"Girl, I don't know what to say except everything will be all right. It might not seem like that now, but it will. One way or the other. Everything does happen for a reason. For every good, there is bad, and vice versa. You've got to pray to get on with your life, regardless of what the outcome is. I know it's hard, but trust me, you'll be fine."

"You know, it's funny how yesterday, I was so depressed and feeling like I couldn't make it without Larry, but today when I woke up, I actually started picturing what it would be like to be single again. I guess I was trying to face reality. Although, I still don't fully understand why he's doing what he's doing. I mean, whatever happened to 'for better or worse' and 'til death due us part'? We've only been married for two years and look at us. We're already preparing for divorce court."

"Girl, you don't know if you're going to have to get a divorce or not, so don't even start thinking like that."

"Well, it sure seems like that's what he wants. Normally, I never think the worst about anything. You're usually the pessimistic one when it comes to situations like this, but I'm optimistic about everything. And although I never really thought about it before, that one saying you have makes a lot of sense."

"Which saying is that? You know I have a lot of them," Karen said, laughing, trying to brighten Regina's spirits.

"Yeah, you do," Regina said softly. "But I'm talking about the one where you say, 'If you expect the worse, you won't be disappointed when something bad happens.' Actually, it's a good way to think, because Lord knows, I've gotten my feelings hurt more than a few times by expecting everything to turn out perfect."

Karen turned into her subdivision and passed the Ridgemore East sign. As she drove closer to her house, she saw a black vehicle parked in the driveway.

Regina looked at her and burst out laughing. "Were you expecting company or something?"

"No," Karen said, shaking her head. "Sometimes I just can't believe John. He just won't give it a rest."

"Girl, what do you expect? You're his wife, and this is where he lives. He'd be a fool not to try and make things right with you. I've told you before, you'd better let the man move back in there, before you end up like me. All alone."

Karen pursed her lips. "Please. I spent a couple of hours with him yesterday, when I got back from taking Mom out to dinner. I told him that maybe I would see him again this weekend, and here he is less than a day later."

"Yeah, and as I recall, when we were driving back home last night, you had a big smile on your face. You were glad to be with him, and you know it. You might as well let him move back in, because all you're doing is trying to play hard to get."

"He still hasn't gone to any Gamblers Anonymous meetings, and there's no way I'm trusting him to quit this on his own," Karen said, reaching toward the backseat to pick up her purse. She opened the car door and stepped out.

Regina walked around to the driver's side. "Well, have fun, and please, by all means, do everything you *know* I would do."

"Girl, please. It's not even like that."

"Oh, yes it is."

"Are you gonna be okay?" Karen asked, backing away from the car.

"Yeah, I guess."

"Oh, no. We were supposed to get something to eat."

"Yeah, I know, but since we didn't make it to the health club to work out, I'm not really hungry, and this whole evening has ruined what little bit of an appetite I had, anyway."

"Yeah, I know what you mean. Oh well, I'd better get in here to see what's up with John. I'll call you later when he leaves."

"Are you kidding? I'll bet he's planning to spend the

night. How long have you made him go without sex, anyway? If I were you, I'd be giving him some."

"Bye, Regina."

"SO, WHAT ARE YOU doing here?" Karen asked, plopping down on the sofa in the great room. John was sitting on the other end, smiling at her. The television was on, and it was obvious that he'd made himself right at home. He'd even taken his shoes off and propped his feet up on the coffee table—something he knew he wasn't supposed to be doing.

"I stopped by to get the electric drill, so I figured I'd wait for you to get home."

"Yeah, right," she said skeptically. "What do you need the drill for?"

"My mother wants me to hang some mini-blinds for her, and there's too many screws to do it manually."

Let her buy her own drill. That's what Karen wanted to tell him, but since she'd be talking about his mother, she decided to keep it to herself. "So when are you going to put them up?"

"Probably tomorrow when I get off work. You must've ridden with Regina to the health club?"

"Yeah, I rode with her, but we never got there."

"Why not?"

"She decided to take a detour over to Marilyn's to see if Larry was there, and sure enough, he was."

"They didn't get into it, did they?"

"Hmmph. More than that. She threw a rock through his car window."

"Not the Lexus!"

"Yeah, and you know how strung out he is on that stupid car. He was pissed. And had the audacity to push her."

"What?" John said, raising his eyebrows.

"He sure did. I've never seen him act like this before. It's like he's a totally different person. If I didn't know better, I'd swear he was on drugs."

"Well, actually, I'm not surprised that he's messing around."

"Why not?"

"Because whenever we've gone to see the Bears or the Bulls, his eyes were always wandering. But he never tried to come on to anybody, so I never thought he'd go this far. And especially with somebody you guys are friends with."

"Shit, Marilyn was never a friend of mine. I tried to warn Regina about her from the very beginning, but she wouldn't listen. I knew Marilyn was jealous of her, and that's why I've always used a long-handled spoon whenever I've had to deal with her. I knew she couldn't be trusted. And how come you never told me he was looking at other women all the time?"

"That was his business, not mine, and I told you, he never came on to anybody in front of me, so I never thought it was any big deal."

"Well, as you can see, it was a big deal."

"Larry should be ashamed of himself. I could never see myself doing anything like that."

"I hope not, because if you did I'd kill you," she said, throwing the tan-colored jacquard pillow at him.

"Although I don't see why I'm *not* looking for someone else. You don't want me."

"John, please. You know that's not why I asked you to move out. This is strictly about your gambling and nothing else."

"Yeah, but we could have worked this out without me having to leave."

"You've been doing this for almost three months now, and when you didn't come home on time for my birthday, that pushed me over the edge. I was practically begging you to get some help, but you refused. My hands were tied. Over and over, you kept singing the same song, that you weren't going to bet on the horses anymore, but you kept doing it anyway. We may not have the same problem that Regina and Larry are having, but to me it's just as serious. Financial problems can shatter any relationship, and that's exactly what was happening to us. So, we need this time apart."

"What good is it doing?"

"You tell me? It's supposed to make you take a long look at what you're doing to our marriage. So, is it?"

"I was aware of what I was doing before I moved out, and I told you I'm not going to do that anymore. If I wasn't serious, would I have deposited over half my paycheck into the account last Friday?"

"I don't know, because you brought all of your money home the week before my birthday, and then you still threw your whole paycheck away the very next week. You can put on a front for only so long, but when you have a problem, you just can't keep it going. I don't understand why you can't see that."

"What if I start going to the meetings? Will that satisfy you enough for us to get on with our lives?"

"Only if you're sincere about it. You have to want to go for yourself, otherwise it's not even worth the trouble."

"Fine," John said in frustration. "I'll go to the meetings. I'll call to find out when the next one is, tomorrow."

"That's all I've been asking you to do from the very beginning."

"Have you had anything to eat?"

"No. Regina and I were supposed to go get something, but with everything that went on, we never got around to it. She didn't have an appetite, anyway. Which is another reason I'm really worried about her. She seems like she's trying to accept what's going on, but I know deep down, she's in a lot of pain."

"Maybe you should keep a close eye on her. You never know how something like this can affect a person. And you know how sensitive Regina is."

"Yeah, I know. I told her I'd give her a call later on after you left."

"I was thinking maybe I could spend the night," he said slyly. "It's already after seven-thirty, and one night isn't going to hurt anything. It's not like I don't live here."

Regina had been right, Karen thought. He'd been planning to spend the night all along and had been setting her up for the kill the entire time. "I don't know," she said, pulling her legs up on the couch under her behind. "I don't think we're ready for that."

"Of course we are. You still love me, don't you?" he said, pulling her closer to him.

She didn't resist. "You know I do, but that doesn't have anything to do with this. The last thing I want is for us to get back together before this problem is taken care of."

"I promise, I'll start going to the meetings," he said, turning her toward him. He kissed her on her forehead.

She couldn't believe she was letting him do this. She'd tried to be hard about all of this so he would get the picture, but like always, he knew what it took to get next to her. The man was smooth, and he knew it. It was almost like they were playing some kind of game or something. She'd made him move out, and here he was spending the night at his own house with his own wife. The more she thought about it, the sillier it seemed. Although, this was the first time she'd gotten him to agree to go to those support group meetings, so really, not all of her efforts had been lost. She'd let him spend the night tonight, but wouldn't authorize his moving back in until she saw some real progress with his gambling obsession. And since he just so happened to be spending the night, she didn't see any reason to disappoint Regina. She was going to make love to her husband.

CHAPTER 14

It was Friday at 9 a.m. and the last time Karen had spoken with Regina was Wednesday evening. She'd been worried sick about her all week, but with John staying over the last few nights, she hadn't found much time to check on her. The girl hadn't made one single attempt to go into work ever since that terrible incident over at Marilyn's four days ago. On Monday, it had seemed like she was coming to terms with the whole Larry and Marilyn situation, but as the week had gone on, Regina had become more and more depressed. Something was going to have to be done. That was all there was to it. She wasn't about to let her girl go out like this. Not without a serious fight.

Karen closed her office door, moved back around her desk, and sat down. She was wearing a cream-colored silk blouse and a magenta crepe skirt. She was planning to take the afternoon off and hadn't wanted to be bothered with wearing a suit today. Plus, she usually dressed a little more casual on Fridays, anyway.

She dialed Regina's number.

"Hello?" Regina answered, sounding as if she'd been asleep when the phone had rung.

"Hey, girl. Wake up."

Regina groaned. "Hey."

"So, I see you stayed home from work again."

"Mmm-hmm. I'm just not in the mood for dealing with anybody."

"Well, you'd better get in the mood. You haven't been out of the house all week, and I'm putting an end to that little routine, today."

"Girl, please. I'm not going anywhere. There's nowhere to go. Nowhere I want to go."

Karen was at a loss for words. This girl was sounding so down and out that you'd have thought the world had come to an end. She had to think of something quick. "Look, Regina. Since I'm taking the afternoon off, you and I are driving over to the mall to do some shopping. I need to find a couple of shorts sets for Memorial Day weekend, anyway. So, after I run home and throw on a pair of jeans, I'll be by your house to pick you up no later than two o'clock. And I'm not taking no for an answer."

Regina exhaled deeply. "I don't feel like it."

"Since when don't you feel like going shopping? And I can't remember a time when you didn't feel like spending some money? Please. Just be dressed by two o'clock.

You'll feel a lot better once you take a nice, hot bath and put on one of your many outfits that still have the price tag on it."

"Girl, why are you doing this? I won't be any fun. You'll have a much better time if you go by yourself."

"I'll pick you up at two. Okay?"

"I guess. You're sure you're only wearing a pair of jeans and a sweatshirt, right? 'Cause I don't feel like getting dressed up. These days, you know I can't stand that."

"I laid my jeans out before I left for work this morning, so you don't have to worry about me getting dressed up. It's bad enough that I have to do it all week long. I'm late for my meeting, so I'll see you this afternoon, okay?"

"All right. Talk to you later."

REGINA HAD dropped back off to sleep after she'd hung up from talking to Karen, and now it was almost noon. She sat up on the edge of the bed and pressed against the sides of her head with both hands. She had a headache out of this world and felt like she hadn't had one hour of sleep.

She dragged herself into the bathroom, plugged the drain in the tub, and started her bathwater. She poured in two capfuls of pink bubble bath. She turned around to face the mirror and frowned when she saw how horrible her face looked. She'd skipped every aspect of her usual skincare regimen all week, and now ugly, red splotches were plastered across her cheeks. How was she going to go anywhere looking like this? She'd heard one of the supermodels on TV saying that whenever her skin broke out, she smoothed Listerine over it. At the time, Regina had thought it sounded crazy, but right now, she was ready and willing to try anything.

She scrubbed her face with the Mary Kay cleanser she'd purchased from a girl at work, then patted Listerine across her cheeks with a cotton ball. She pulled off her nightgown, turned off the scorching hot water, and eased her body into the sudsy bubbles. It was a little hotter than she liked, but her body was slowly starting to adapt to it. She went to reach for her wash towel on the side of the tub and stopped when she felt a spell of dizziness. She sat still with her eyes closed and waited a couple of minutes for it to pass. Maybe the water was too hot. Or maybe she was having problems with anemia again. Last year, she'd had to take pills for almost five months before the iron in her body had finally regained its proper level. It was a good thing she'd scheduled her yearly exam for tomorrow; otherwise she might have had to wait until sometime next week just to get in and see her doctor.

Although she was hardly looking forward to having one of those miserable pap smears. The procedure was painless, but the thought of having an almost total stranger stick some chilly metal instrument inside her made her uneasy. And no matter how many times she experienced it, the feeling never got any better. After tomorrow, though, a pap smear would be the least of her worries for at least the next twelve months.

She rubbed the Zest soap across the water-drenched washcloth, washed herself from the shoulders down, and crinkled her nose. She'd gone three whole days without cleaning any part of her body, and if Karen hadn't insisted that she go shopping with her, today would have been number four. This didn't make a lick of sense. She needed to be ashamed of herself. But for some odd reason she wasn't. She just didn't care. As far as she was concerned, there was no one she had to impress, because with the exception of a marriage certificate filed away in a safety-deposit box, there was no sign of a husband, anyway.

After soaking and relaxing for almost a half hour, she thoroughly lathered her body a second time. Just because she didn't seem to have a problem with being a filthy pig, that wasn't reason enough for Karen to have to put up with smelling any horrible scents. She stood up, reached for the bath towel, and carefully dried her pitiful self off. Then she brushed the plaque from her teeth and gargled with blue mouthwash. She walked out into the bedroom, over to the closet, and pulled a pair of stonewashed jeans and a Bulls T-shirt off their hangers. From the dresser drawer, she pulled out a purple bra and matching bikini panties, and slipped both pieces on. She glanced down at her legs and saw that they were already starting to get ashy, but she wasn't in the mood for rubbing any lotion on them. It was a good thing she was wearing socks and jeans—they would conceal it.

Standing in front of the mirror, she tucked in her T-shirt, zipped her pants, and buckled her black Coach belt, which had to be pulled two holes tighter. She'd lost a tremendous amount of weight, thanks to worrying herself to death about Larry. She looked in the mirror and saw what a mess her hair was in. There hadn't been a comb, brush or curling iron near it since she'd locked herself in the house four days ago, and it felt like straw. She went into the bathroom, rubbed some pink moisturizer lotion between the palms of her hands, saturated her hair with it, and brushed her short mane toward the back until every strand was in place. She was far from winning a prize for best hairstyle, but at least she'd look somewhat presentable once she threw on her Bulls baseball cap. Large, gold hoop earrings would add some style to it as well.

After applying foundation, pressed face powder, and a trivial amount of gingersnap blush, her cheeks didn't appear to look so bad after all. Her newfound facial remedy was actually working, and the Bozo look was gone. Thank God for that.

She gathered her purse and her last, partially empty pack of Capri menthol 120s and headed downstairs to the patio. After kicking this disgusting, addictive habit five months ago, she'd been forced to start it up again, even though it had been the one New Year's resolution she'd been able to keep. She'd been sneaking one here and there ever since the night she'd flown back from Atlanta, and although she hated to admit it, the number per day was gradually increasing. Pretty soon, she'd be lighting up the moment her eyelids popped open every morning if she continued at the rate she was going. And she didn't even want to think about all the times she'd raced through the parking lot at work, just to steal a few nicotine puffs. That smoke-free environment at work had made her life a living hell before she'd finally kicked the habit, and she had no idea how she was going to deal with that all over again. This thing with Larry had been far too much for her to handle, and these tiny, little cancer sticks were the only crutch she had to hold on to. They were the reason she'd been able to keep at least some sanity and why her nerves, at least for the most part, were somewhat settled. Larry had always hated the fact that she smoked. Said it wasn't ladylike, that it was hazardous to her health. Karen, on the other hand, was more concerned with the dangers of secondhand smoke. As usual, that girl was worried about herself.

Regina smiled at her latest thought and then sat down on the bluish-green lounger. She stretched out, lit a cigarette, took a long drag, and blew it out. She felt better already. These Capris were much skinnier and a lot more feminine-looking than any of the other brands on the market, and they probably weren't nearly as risky. And even if they were, it made her feel a lot less guilty by pretending that they weren't.

After inhaling a couple more drags, she tapped the cigarette with her finger, and the butt fell into the ashtray next to her. She closed her eyes. It was funny how she hadn't wanted to go shopping when Karen had called, but now she was looking forward to it. And come to think of it, she wasn't feeling the slightest bit depressed. Maybe it was the nicotine. But then, maybe it was her prayers finally being answered. Either way, she felt better than she had in what seemed like an eternity.

"GIRL, LOOK AT THIS," Regina said, leaning over a diamond-filled showcase. They were in one of the fine jewelry stores housed in the lower level of the mall.

"Oooh, that's sharp," Karen said, leaning forward to catch a glimpse. "How much is it?"

"I don't know, but who cares. Just look at it."

Shoot, Karen had wanted Regina to get out of the house and have a good time, but not this good a time. So far, they'd only gone to one store, and she'd already bought two linen blazers, a coatdress, and a business suit, without even trying any of it on. She'd spent over five hundred dollars and appeared to be just getting started. Maybe shopping hadn't been the best choice for an outing.

"Yeah, it's nice, but I can tell just by looking at it that it's way too expensive," Karen offered.

"Nothing's too expensive for this Visa I've got sitting here in my wallet. Especially since it's got Larry's name printed all over it. Unfortunately for him, it's one of the few accounts my name isn't on."

Karen didn't say anything.

"Can I help you ladies find something," a classy-looking, forty-something saleslady said, smiling.

"You sure can. I'd like to see that tennis bracelet toward the back of the case."

"This one?" the saleslady asked, pointing to one that looked a lot less expensive than the one Regina was eyeing.

"No, the one over there."

"This one?" the saleslady asked again, pointing to another bracelet.

"Yes, that's the one."

"This is one of our most popular bracelets," the lady said, removing it from the case.

"How much is it?"

"Let's see. It's six thousand five hundred dollars, but we're having a half-off sale, so you'd be looking at about thirty-two fifty, plus tax."

"Hmmm," Regina said, taking the bracelet into her hand and clasping it together around her wrist. "This is really nice. What do you think, Karen?"

"I think it's nice, but didn't you just buy a tennis bracelet earlier this year?"

"Yeah, but that wasn't the one I really wanted, anyway. It's okay, but nothing worth talking about."

What was she saying? If Karen remembered correctly, Regina had spent over $1,200 on that bracelet. And now it wasn't even worth talking about? Once again, the girl was out of control, and Karen didn't have the slightest idea of what to do about it.

"That's a beautiful ring you have on your middle finger. Are those real diamonds?" the saleslady asked. And was serious.

Karen laughed before she knew it because she knew Regina was about to go off.

"What do you mean, are they real diamonds? What else would they be? Hell, if you must know, my husband bought it for me on our first anniversary."

"Oh . . . I . . . I didn't mean anything by it. It's just that nowadays the CZs look just as genuine as the diamonds."

Yeah, right. Who did she think she was fooling? Truth was, she thought two carats were a bit much for a black woman to be wearing. That is, if it was real. Regina rolled her eyes at the woman and scanned a few more bracelets in the showcase. She really wanted the one she had on, but that comment was making her think twice about it.

The saleslady noticed Regina's indecisiveness and spoke up in a hurry. "We do have a layaway plan, if you're interested."

Shit. There was no hope for this woman. As far as Regina could recollect, she hadn't asked about any damn layaway plan. "I'll tell you what," Regina said with wrinkles already formed across her forehead. "You can take this bracelet back, because I don't do layaways, and I sure as hell don't do business with ignorant, prejudiced people like you." She slipped it off and dropped it onto the glass counter.

Regina and Karen left the store without looking back. They were both steaming.

"I don't care how many college degrees you get, how much money you make, or how nice a neighborhood you live in, you're still just another black face to some white people," Karen said.

"I can't believe that wench asked me about some lay-away plan. And to think she wanted to know if my diamonds were real," Regina said, switching her clothing bag from her right hand to her left one.

They continued down the mall toward the other jewelry store.

"It just goes to show, some things never change. Don't get me wrong. Not all white people are like that, because I've got two close friends from where I used to work who treat me no different than anybody else. And you know how down-to-earth my nail tech is. But there are always going to be those certain ones who have all blacks stereotyped the same way," Karen said, taking notice of the cookie shop they were passing by. She decided against going in it, though.

"I swear. You'd never know it was 1995 with the way some white people act."

"No, really you wouldn't."

"Shit like that makes me want to hurt somebody," Regina said.

"Yeah, I know, but what sense would it make for you to be sitting behind bars, when the rest of this racist world would still be out here doing their thing."

They stopped in front of the jewelry store that they'd been forced to take their business to. A nice-looking, immaculately dressed black man, probably in his early thirties, was standing behind the counter.

"Well, well, well," Regina said, turning to look at Karen. "I guess we don't have to worry about any stereotyping up in here, now do we?"

Karen laughed. "Girl, shut up, and let's go in."

"Good afternoon, ladies," the salesman said as they entered the store.

"Hello," Regina and Karen said in unison.

"Is there something you're looking for in particular?" he asked, smiling.

"Actually, there is," Regina answered. "I'd like to see your diamond tennis bracelets."

"If you'll follow me over here, I'll show them to you."

Regina set her bag down when they arrived at the next showcase. She spotted the one she was interested in almost immediately and pointed toward it. "Could I see that one?"

"Sure." He pulled the bracelet out and, unlike the previous salesclerk, placed it around her wrist and clasped it for her.

"Yeah, this is nice," Regina said. "What do you think about this one?" she continued, gearing the question toward Karen.

"It's just as sharp as the other one, and it seems like it's the same weight as the other one too. I like it."

"What's the price on this one?" Regina asked him.

"We've got a fifty-percent-off sale going on, so it would be half of the price on the tag," he said.

That was typical, Karen thought. Whenever one jewelry store in the mall had a sale, the others always seemed to follow suit. Had to, though, to be competitive, she guessed.

He lifted the price tag. "It's seven thousand dollars, so the sale price is thirty-five hundred."

"Hmmm. That's two-fifty more than the one I just looked at down the mall," Regina said. She was going to buy it regardless, but there was no sense in letting him know too soon. If she held out long enough, maybe he'd meet his competitor's price.

He didn't say anything.

And neither did Regina.

Karen was at the other end of the store, browsing the watches.

"This bracelet is definitely you," he said.

"Yeah, I really like it, but two-fifty is two-fifty," Regina said, unsnapping the bracelet.

"What if I meet the other store's price? Will you buy it then?"

"I sure will."

"Fine, let me take it over here, so I can ring you up."

Regina passed her credit card across the counter as Karen walked toward her. "So, you decided to get it, huh?"

"I sure did."

"So, where do you want to go now?" Karen asked.

"I'm with you. You still have to find an outfit, don't you?"

"Yeah. I was thinking about going into Field's, and although Nordstrom is probably too expensive, I want to check out what they have too."

"I need to go into Field's anyway, because there's this red Coach handbag I've been wanting to—"

"Excuse me, I don't mean to interrupt, but I need to get your signature on the dotted line," the salesman said.

"Oh, I'm sorry. I was so busy talking, I wasn't paying attention," Regina said.

He slipped her receipt inside the plastic drawstring bag and handed it to her. "Thanks for shopping with us. I hope you enjoy it."

"It's such a beautiful bracelet that you can't help but enjoy it," Regina said.

"A beautiful bracelet for a beautiful lady," he said.

Regina smiled. When she stepped outside the store, she couldn't help but look back to see if he was still watching her, and he was. She smiled again and kept walking until they were out of his sight.

"I haven't seen you blush like that since—"

"Since the time I met Larry. Shit, what can I say, that brother back there looked good."

Karen waited for Regina to add the part about him being dark, but she didn't.

"Yeah, he was definitely nice looking, but you're still married, my dear."

"Hmmph. By paperwork only."

"Whoa. What's up with you?"

"Nothing, except I'm finally starting to wake up. I thought I was doing fine on Monday, but then I got depressed all over again after that incident over at Marilyn's. But today I feel good and like I can get on with my life. It's only been two weeks since he walked out, but a lot has happened, and I've been doing some serious praying. The best thing you could have done was call me this morning, because I really needed to get out of that house. But, as usual, you always know the right thing to do when it comes to me and my problems."

"I've been praying for you myself, and I'm glad you're feeling a lot better."

They walked through Marshall Field's cosmetics entrance.

"I know you're not serious about getting another Coach, are you?" Karen asked Regina in disbelief.

"Oh, yes I am."

"Girl, if you keep it up, you're going to spend five thousand dollars before we even leave here."

"Shit, that's what I'm planning on doing anyway. You can even charge that shorts set if you want to. And after we leave the mall, I need you to stop by my bank, so I can request a five-thousand-dollar cash advance."

"Girl, what are you going to do with five thousand dollars cash? Larry is still paying the bills like he said, isn't he?"

"Yeah. But so what? All I know is that this Visa of his has a ten-thousand-dollar credit line, and I'm going to charge up every dime of it. Shit. Let him do some worrying for a change."

"Girl, he's going to die when he gets that bill next month."

"Maybe. But to tell you the honest truth, I really don't give a damn.

CHAPTER 15

A FTER SCRUBBING THE TUB and sink in the master bath-
room, Karen removed a pair of white rubber gloves
from her hands, rinsed them off, hung them from the
shower nozzle to dry, and walked into the bedroom.
Merry Maids cleaned the house once every two weeks,
but this didn't happen to be one of them. She'd thought
about increasing the number of visits, but right now, that
didn't seem logical, with John gambling the way he was.
The budget was tight enough, and all she'd be doing was
making things harder for herself in the long run.

She sat down on the bed and wondered if he'd gone to
that meeting last night like he'd promised. He hadn't
gone any other nights during the week, but that was her
fault. She'd allowed him to sleep over Monday through
Thursday, and it was obvious that he no longer saw an
incentive to go. The man had gotten too comfortable for

his own good, which is why she'd had to put her foot down when she'd spoken to him yesterday afternoon: No more sleepovers until he was consistently going to those Gamblers Anonymous meetings.

She hated to call his mother's house, but she needed to know if he'd done what he was supposed to. She dialed the number without even thinking about it. It was funny how she never used this number unless it was absolutely necessary but knew it well enough not to have to look it up. But then, for as long as she could remember, she'd never forgotten any phone number that she'd dialed at least once. Her memory for numbers was strong, and that was probably why she'd been so successful with a career in finance.

"Hello?" John's mother said.

Shoot, she'd been hoping John would answer, because she wasn't in the mood for dealing with this woman who was already sounding like she was mad at the world. "Hi, how are you?" Karen asked out of courtesy.

"Fine. I'm on a long-distance phone call, so you'll have to call back. I think John is asleep, anyway." Click.

Oooh. She'd switched back over to her other conversation without as much as saying, "Bye, I'll tell him you called, I'll tell him to call you," or anything. Karen slammed the phone on the hook. That woman made her sick, and she had better be damned glad that Karen's mother had taught her early on to respect her elders. She didn't know how John was putting up with the old bat. Living with a mother like that was something she wouldn't have wished on an enemy. John was a good one. Much better than she could have been, that was for sure.

She picked up the phone again to dial Regina until she remembered her saying her yearly physical was scheduled for nine-thirty. What a terrible way to start a Saturday morning, Karen thought, but better she than her.

After straightening the covers on her bed, vacuuming every room on the upstairs level, and throwing a load of clothes in the washing machine, she sat down in the great room and dialed John again.

"Hello?" It was her again.

"Hi, is John there?" Karen said, trying to keep her composure.

John's mother sighed deeply. "I don't see whatcha callin' him for. The best thang you coulda done was put him out. He just don't know it yet. See, I knew this day was comin' from the very beginning."

Karen didn't want to get into it with this woman, so she ignored her. "Do you mind if I speak to John, please?"

"If he had only listened to me and not married you. Lord knows he wouldn't be going through anythang like this."

She was trying Karen's patience, and Karen didn't know how much more of this she could stand without blowing up. "Look, Mrs. Jackson, are you going to let me speak to him or not?"

"Let me tell you one thang, my baby will always have a place to stay as long as I'm breathin'. He's much better off with me anyway. Why don't you just leave him alone?"

This woman was sounding like some crazy person and, the more Karen thought about it, like a jealous girl-friend. She was acting as if she were in some kind of competition with her son's own wife. Karen wished she would get a life, keep her bossy self out of their business, and figure out that her "baby" was thirty-nine and not five. If she didn't, she was going to get her feelings hurt. This thing with respecting elders could only go so far.

Karen was just about to hang up when she heard John in the background asking who was on the phone. When his mother didn't answer him, he went and picked up another extension. "Karen?"

"Yeah, it's me."

"Mama, you can hang up now," John said. "I've got it."

She didn't budge.

"Mama, I said you can hang up," he repeated. Impatience flowed through his voice. He was clearly upset.

She blasted the phone on the hook, and Karen smiled. That's what his mother got for meddling in other folks' business. Served her right. She'd needed to be put in her place from the moment Karen had called, and she was glad John had taken care of it.

"You think we can spend the day together?" John asked, chomping at the bit.

"I'm fine. How are you?" Karen said, laughing.

He laughed too. "How are you, baby? I didn't mean to

be rude, but I don't want to waste any time. I want to be over there by noon."

"Did you go to your meeting last night?"

John paused. Whenever he did that, it meant his reply wasn't going to be promising. "Well, actually, I didn't, because I fell asleep, and when I woke up, it was too late."

Karen's spirits dropped instantly. He just didn't mean to take care of this problem of his. How was she ever going to get through to him? After all this, he was still blowing the whole thing off like it wasn't serious. Now she was wondering if he'd gone to the track yesterday. "So, what did you do yesterday? I mean, where did you go after work? And you know what I'm talking about."

"I didn't go play the horses, if that's what you mean. I didn't deposit any money in the checking account, but I've got $700 cash here to give you today."

Oh, now he was going to use money as an excuse to see her. She couldn't believe he'd even stoop low enough to try something like that. But it was working, though. "You promised you'd go to a meeting, John. And since when do you fall asleep that early on a Friday evening? You haven't done that since I've been married to you."

"I was bored, I guess. I didn't have anything to do. You said I couldn't spend the night with you, so I came to my mother's and fell asleep. That was that."

"Can't you see that if you don't do this, you're going

to be right back out there messing up your money again?"

"Let's talk about it when I get there."

She'd known that was coming. Especially since she was cornering him between two walls. He never liked that. "Fine, but you're not spending the night, so don't even plan on it."

He didn't even acknowledge that last comment. "I'll see you around noon. You want me to pick up something for lunch?"

"It's too early for me. But we can pick up something later if you want."

"I'll see you then."

"I can't believe you're still runnin' behind that woman after she put you out the way she did," John's mother screamed out in the background. She'd obviously been listening to his conversation all along and had been waiting for the opportune time to throw her two cents in.

"Look, Mama. Karen is my wife, and I'm sick of you disrespecting her. Don't make me choose between you and my wife, because if you do, you won't like the outcome. I'm sick of every time I turn around, you're sticking your nose into my business. This is going to have to stop. I'm not some little kid."

Ha, ha, and double ha, ha. This was getting good, and Karen was loving every bit of what she was hearing. "Hey. I'll see you when you get here," she said and hung up the phone. She laughed so hard that she fell back on the sofa. She lay there cracking up for two whole minutes.

A S USUAL, John was looking casually fine. Karen smiled as she watched him step out of the BMW and walk toward the garage, which was already open. He was dressed in a beige, short-sleeved pullover by Perry Ellis, a pair of perfectly starched Silvertab Levi's, and a pair of black, toe-enclosed huarache sandals. She shook her head in amazement. It was strange how so many positive aspects could be wrapped up in one man. A gorgeous face, skin like a baby's, a size thirty-two waist, and the best sense of humor. Not to mention the fact that he dressed impeccably and always smelled good. It was nothing for him to dish out fifty to sixty dollars for a bottle of cologne to replenish his expensive stock of fragrances, and when it came to a piece of clothing, price was no object as long as he was sure he'd look good in it. But then, it was that same reasoning that was the cause of their separation. If only he could value a dollar the same as his physical characteristics. If he did, he'd be batting a thousand.

John entered through the kitchen and went into the great room, where Karen was standing. He walked over to her.

"Hey, baby," he said, hugging her, then kissing her on the lips.

"Hey," she said. It felt so good to be in his arms. She'd

just seen the man two days ago, but it felt like two weeks. Gosh, she wished he would take those GA meetings more seriously so they could get their marriage back on track, because this current situation was too unstable for her. His visits were starting to feel like those of some boyfriend dropping in to see how his new girlfriend was doing.

"Damn," he said, stepping away from her. "You're looking especially fine this afternoon. Is that new?" he asked, checking her out from head to toe.

"I bought the shirt yesterday when Regina and I went shopping, and you know I've had these jeans forever." She was wearing a sleeveless indigo jean shirt, a pair of comfortably snug Guess jeans, and a pair of metallic-gold slip-on sandals.

"So, what's up for today?" he asked. "You want to go to a movie or something?" He sat down on the sofa, picked up the Saturday edition of the *Daily Herald*, and started skimming through it.

"I guess we could. Although I don't know if anything good is playing or not." She sat down on the love seat adjacent to him and rested her foot on the edge of it. "I want to talk to you first, though, before we go."

He didn't say anything and didn't look up from the paper, which meant he had a pretty good idea where the conversation was headed.

"What I want to know is when you plan on going to a meeting? I hate to keep pressuring you, but you know you have to do this."

"I think there's one tomorrow evening, so I'll probably try to catch that one."

"Try?" She didn't like his choice of words.

"You know what I mean. Don't even worry about it. I'll go."

"You've been claiming that all week, and still you haven't gotten there yet. I just don't understand you. Gambling is no different than alcohol or drugs. Once it becomes an addiction, you have to seek outside help. You can't do this alone, because if you could, you wouldn't be throwing away large sums of money like you do."

"I haven't gone to the track in over two weeks now, and you know it."

"Yeah, only because I asked you to move out. But if I said you could move back in today, you'd be at that track first thing next Friday, right after work."

"No, I wouldn't. I've given that whole gambling thing up. You just don't believe it," he said, setting the paper down, leaning to one side on the sofa, and pulling out the brown leather wallet Karen had bought him last Christmas.

She'd been sort of skeptical when he'd said he had $700 left from the paycheck he'd received yesterday. It had almost been too good to be true, but now, he was actually about to give it to her, and suddenly she felt a huge amount of relief.

"Here's the money for you to deposit," he said, passing her a stack of one-hundred-dollar bills folded in half.

She put it on the glass coffee table, pretending like it was no big deal, though what she really wanted to do was count them. But then, that would look like she didn't trust him, so she decided against it. On a more positive note, though, these one-hundred-dollar bills meant she wouldn't have to make another unnecessary withdrawal from the credit union. "Thanks."

"Why don't you just admit it, I'm a good person," he said, going back to the paper. "How many men do you know would still be giving their wives money to pay bills, even though they've been kicked out of the house? Most people would think I'm some kind of fool."

"I don't know why they would, because you own fifty percent of everything we have, just like I do. And just because you're not staying here doesn't mean you don't have any responsibility. I mean, it's not like I'm taking your money and spending it on myself. I'm using this money to pay the bills that we've both made," she said, staring at him. She was starting to get upset.

"Shit, you don't have to get mad about it," he said irritably. "I was just making a point."

She didn't say anything, because he didn't sound anything like the man who'd been in beg mode for the past three weeks. He was upset. And anyway, he was probably right when he said most men wouldn't give their wives any money, although she didn't see any reason to let him know that she agreed with him.

He dropped the last section of the newspaper next to him on the sofa. "It's still too early to catch a matinee, so let's go get something to eat. I'm starving."

That was just like him to carry on as if there hadn't

been one ounce of tension between the two of them just a minute ago, and since she didn't feel like arguing anyway, she followed his lead. "That's fine, but I want to wait until the mailman gets here, so I can check the bank statement. When I called the automated teller last night, the bank's balance seemed to be way off from the one in the checkbook. He should be here in a few minutes, though. Then we can leave."

"Is there anything good in the refrigerator?" he asked, heading into the kitchen. "I at least need something to tide me over."

"Some juice and a few cold cuts. That's about it. I haven't gone grocery shopping since you moved out."

"What else is new," he said, laughing. "Doesn't make any sense to buy any food, if you don't plan on cooking it."

"Shut up," she said and chuckled.

He came back into the great room with a couple of slices of ham between two pieces of wheat bread and a full glass of Sunny Delight.

"I know this is probably not the time to bring this up and it's probably the last thing you want to hear, but it's something I've been thinking about a lot lately."

He was sounding too serious for her, and she could only imagine what he was preparing to say. "What?"

"I think we should reconsider our decision about not having any kids. I mean, I think we'd make great parents. We've got all this love between us, and we wouldn't have any problems financially either."

Karen frowned and wondered where he'd pulled that big bright idea from. His butt? He had to be kidding. "Have you lost your mind? You knew how I felt about having children from the moment you met me, and I'm sorry to tell you, nothing has changed. And you know I had my tubes sealed off, anyway."

"Yeah, but remember when we had that consultation with your gynecologist and he said that securing those clips around your tubes was the best method because that way, he could go in and surgically remove them if we changed our minds?"

"Please. I don't care if he *can* remove them. The bottom line is, I don't want any children. I'm already thirty and my career is just now starting to take off. I didn't struggle to get a master's degree while working full-time for nothing." This was pissing her off.

"I just think we need something like that. If we had a baby, I probably wouldn't have started on this gambling spree. I need something else to devote my time to."

"A baby isn't some play toy that you can simply pick up when you get bored and put down when you've got something better to do. What about all the times we grab our keys and leave the house at the spur of the moment? We wouldn't be able to do that anymore if we had a baby. Instead, we'd have to be scrounging around for some babysitter. And the last thing I want to do is hightail it to some day care by five-thirty, trying to make sure we don't have to pay a whole dollar for each minute thereafter. I just can't see it. Plus, who has a hundred dollars a week to pay them in the first place? I know we don't."

"I get off work before you do, so I can pick the baby up every day. And the day-care costs wouldn't be a problem if we stop doing some of the other things we do."

"Like what? Because I know you're not prepared to give up Claiborne, Perry Ellis, and Kenneth Cole. And although I don't buy as much designer stuff as you do, I like living comfortably. Living on the edge isn't my thing. What if we had a baby now? Do you think you could have gone out and thrown whole paychecks away like you did? I don't think so."

"If it would mean having a baby, I would give up clothes and everything else."

"That's easy to say right now, but reality is a whole different thing. Plus, I don't want to be tied down with any kids. I watched my mother struggle to take care of me and Sheila when my father conveniently walked out, and if she hadn't been the excellent money manager that she was, I don't know where we'd be. That's never going to happen to me."

"I know it's never going to happen to you, because I would never walk out on you. The only reason I moved out this time is because you insisted. I'm telling you, I love you too much to do anything like that. You mean everything to me, so I don't understand how you would even think something like that?"

"My parents meant everything to each other too, but look what my father did. There're just no guarantees. My grandmother used to say all the time that you never know what tomorrow might bring, and she was right. I'm sorry, but getting pregnant and having a baby isn't for me."

"Well, at least think about it," he said, setting the near empty plate on the floor. "Okay?"

"There's nothing to think about," she said, turning away from him. "This is a dead issue as far as I'm concerned. If you wanted someone to lie around in the house barefoot and pregnant, you should have married someone else, because I'm just not the one."

"I didn't want to marry anybody else. I fell in love with you."

"Look, I can't change who I am or how I feel." She stood up when she thought she heard the mailman.

John flicked on the television set. "Fine, Karen. If that's the way you feel."

After retrieving the mail, she came back and sat on the love seat, where she shuffled through each piece until she found the monthly statement from Bank First. She dropped everything else onto the coffee table. She opened the envelope and pulled out four pages. The first two summarized the checking account and the last two were for savings. She scanned down the first page and didn't see any errors. But when she came to the second page, she noticed two withdrawals, each in the amount of $500. She frowned. That just couldn't be. She hadn't used her Cirrus card to withdraw that kind of money since she could remember, and as far as she knew, $500 was over and above the daily limit for automatic teller withdrawals. She wasn't sure, but she thought the maximum was somewhere in the neighborhood of two hundred fifty. And since John never carried the checkbook, the only way he could have done something like this was by going to the bank and making a teller withdrawal. For his sake, that had better not be the case.

"Did you make two five-hundred-dollar withdrawals over the past four weeks?"

He didn't answer. His eyes were glued to the television, and she knew he was pretending that he hadn't heard her.

"John!"

"What?" he said, finally looking at her.

"For the second time, did you make two withdrawals over the last four weeks?"

"How much were they for?"

"If you made the got-damn withdrawals, you should already know how much," she yelled.

He dropped his face into the palms of his hands and shook his head from side to side like he didn't know what to say next. "Yeah, I think I did, but that was over two weeks ago."

"Why didn't you tell me? Here I am writing checks like they're going out of style, and you're stealing money out of the account like some child. What if I'd written too many checks and they started bouncing? If I'm not mistaken, I think they charge around twenty dollars for having insufficient funds."

He looked up at her but was speechless.

"I've never bounced a check in my entire life, and I'm not about to start just because of your irresponsible ass. Hell, I work at that bank. I can't believe you. You're not only getting rid of the money you earn, but now you're messing with the money we've got saved at the bank? I should have never told you that I keep an extra thousand dollars in the account for emergencies. Shit, does going to the horse track sound like an emergency situation to you?"

"Look, baby. I'm sorry. That was before I moved out."

"Stop lying. This second withdrawal was *after* you moved out. As a matter of fact, the ninth was on a Tuesday, so that means you were gambling on a weekday."

"I know, but I haven't done anything like that since. I know how stupid that was. You're right about me having a problem, and I swear I'm going to that meeting tomorrow, if that's the last thing I do."

"I really don't care what you do tomorrow, but right now, I want you to get the hell out of here."

"Baby, please. Why are you tripping about something that happened weeks ago? You know I haven't done anything like that since then. We need to spend some time together. For once, can't you just forgive me?"

"Get out!"

"Look—"

"I don't want to hear it. I just want you to get your ass out."

John rose from the sofa, proceeded through the

kitchen, and walked through the garage to his car. He started it up, backed out the wide driveway, and left.

Karen felt like screaming. How could she have been so stupid? It hadn't dawned on her to check for teller withdrawals when she'd tried to check the balance last evening. She should've suspected something like this all along. Drug addicts did this all the time, and she didn't see much difference with someone who was strung out on gambling. She hated him for doing this. Now she'd have to transfer funds from savings to checking in order to cover some of the purchases she'd made yesterday. To her, that was like robbing Peter to pay Paul, and it made her sick to her stomach just thinking about it. Damn. She could understand if he'd done something responsible like getting the transmission fixed or paying a bill, but gambling, uh-uh.

She lifted the handset of the phone and dialed the twenty-four-hour automated teller line. She pressed "3" to select transfer funds, entered in both account numbers, and then the amount, which was $2,500. She wasn't taking any chances on him stealing from this account ever again, and she was going to deposit all of it into her credit union first thing Monday morning.

The system was taking longer than usual to process, so she continued to wait. Finally, it responded. "You do not have sufficient funds available to complete this transaction, please press the star key for more options."

"What?" she said out loud. They had at minimum $2,500 in that account. She just knew he hadn't messed around and withdrawn money from there as well. She picked up the third and fourth pages of the statement and searched down it. Sure enough, there had been a $500 withdrawal. A wave of heat flashed through her body. That brought the total to fifteen hundred. The man was crazy. Had to be, if he was doing some stupid shit like this. Instead of support group meetings, he needed psychiatric help.

She went through the computer-driven procedure again and entered $2,000 as the amount to be transferred, and this time the automated teller accepted it. She hung up and sighed deeply. What if his name had been on her credit union account? He would really have showed his ass then. That was for sure.

She lay back on the love seat and tried to relax. A million thoughts flickered through her mind, but one stood out loud and clear: Instead of paying bills with the $700 he'd just given her, she was going to seriously consider using it to file for a divorce.

CHAPTER 16

"**G**UESS WHO JUST CALLED to say they were on their way over to talk?" Regina asked Karen while taking a puff from her cigarette and repositioning the phone. She hadn't smoked the whole time they'd been shopping yesterday, because she hadn't wanted Karen to know she was strung out again.

"Not Larry, I know."

"He sure did."

"What is it he wants to talk about?"

"I don't know, because he wouldn't say. But I've got a feeling he's come to his senses. He was sounding awfully pleasant. He even went as far as asking me how I've been doing."

"Are you going to take him back?"

"I don't know what to do. A part of me wants to, because quite obviously, I'm still in love with him, but the other part of me says he can't be trusted, and that I should divorce him. I just don't know."

"You have to do whatever you have to do, but I do think you need to think about this further before you make a final decision. He needs to understand that you're the one running the show now, and not him."

"I know that's right. Just yesterday, I was feeling like I could make it just fine without him, and now look at me, sitting here contemplating whether I should take the man back."

"Girl, you're not doing anything that I'm not. I called John at his mother's house this morning, because I really wanted to see him, and when he got here, he started rambling on about having a baby, and then to top that off, my bank statement came in the mail, and I found out he'd made two $500 withdrawals from checking and another for the same amount from savings. A whole fifteen hundred dollars. Can you believe that shit?"

"No!" Regina said. "I know you're lying, aren't you?"

"Oh, no I'm not. The man has lost it, and I'm through with him for good. I threw his ass out of here a couple of hours ago. I'm so pissed off, I don't know what to do, and I'm seriously thinking about filing for a divorce. I just can't take this shit anymore."

"Girl, please. You'd better push that idea right out of your mind, because there is no way you should be throwing your marriage away just like that. And anyway, he hasn't gone gambling since he made those withdrawals, has he?"

"No. At least, not that I know of. He even gave me most of his paycheck when he got here, but that's beside the point, because the bottom line is that he hasn't gone to one of those meetings. Things are not going to get better until he does, but he doesn't seem to understand that."

"Well, at least give him until tomorrow. I mean, I know he's messed up a lot of money, but it seems to me like he's really been trying for the past two weeks."

"Shit, I'm tired of giving him chances, and as far as I'm concerned, he used his last one when he made those withdrawals from our bank accounts. I'm moving every dime out of the bank and into my credit union because there's no telling what he might do as long as he knows he can get cash whenever he wants to."

Regina heard the doorbell ring. "Girl, that's Larry," she said excitedly. "I'll call you as soon as he leaves."

"Good luck, and whatever you do, make sure he understands that he has to dance to your music if he wants you back."

"You know I will. Talk to you later," Regina said and hung up the phone. She walked to the front door, smoothed her hair on each side, and opened the door.

"How's it going?" Larry asked, walking in dressed in a red polo shirt and a pair of black shorts.

"Fine. How are things with you?" she asked, closing the door, following behind him to the family room.

He took a seat on the sofa, and she sat in the oversized chair with her feet pulled partially under her butt. There was complete silence for at least half a minute.

Regina decided to break the ice. "So, what did you want to talk to me about?"

Larry forced his body to the edge of the sofa and clasped his hands together, looking straight ahead and away from Regina, almost as if he had something to say but wasn't sure how to go about it. Finally, he spoke. "I really don't know where to begin."

That was obvious. When he'd phoned, she was certain he'd come to his senses and was planning to beg his way back home, but now she wasn't so sure. He was beating around the bush, and that wasn't like him. But she decided not to jump to any conclusions until she heard exactly what he had to say. She continued to listen.

He breathed deeply. "I guess there's no easy way to do this, so I'll just say what I have to say. I'm in love with Marilyn, we're going to have a baby, and I'm filing for a divorce."

Regina swallowed hard, tightened the muscles in her face, and willfully repressed all of her emotions. She felt paralyzed and numb. Had she heard him right? She replayed what he'd just said to make sure there hadn't been some sort of a mistake with the way she'd understood it. "What did you just say?"

This time, he turned to look at her. "I'm in love with Marilyn, she's pregnant, and we're going to have a baby."

There hadn't been any mistake at all. That bitch was really pregnant, and this motherfucker right here was the cause of it. She couldn't believe he'd had the audacity to bring his low-down ass over there to announce some shit like that in person. But now that he had, she wanted to know how long he'd known about all of this. "How many months is she, Larry?"

"Six weeks. It wasn't something we planned. It just happened. You have to believe that."

"Oh, you mean like when you screwed her for the first time, and it was in our own fuckin' bed? Is that what you mean? Things always seem to 'just be happening' when it comes to you and Marilyn, and to be honest, I don't even want to hear that tired shit anymore."

"Hey, I'm sorry for all of this, but there's nothing I can do to change it. You're just going to have to accept that. The last thing I want to do is argue with you, and the only reason I came over here to tell you in person was because I felt I had a responsibility to do so. I didn't think it was right for you to find out from somebody else or by accident."

"No, that's not what your responsibility was at all. Your responsibility was to stay faithful to your wife, but you chose not to do that. We took vows before God and promised to spend the rest of our lives together, and you disregarded every bit of that. Were things so bad between us that you had to fall for some slut? And how in the hell are you going to be a daddy to some baby when you don't even have what it takes to be a real husband?"

"Why can't we ever sit down and have a civil conversation like two intelligent adults? Damn," he said, grabbing his keys from the table where he had laid them.

"Fuck being civil. It's too late for that shit. You see, while you were lying over there with that little back-stabbing bitch of yours, I was shedding tears, worrying my ass to death, and praying that you would leave her. And to think how stupid I was earlier, thinking you were on your way over here to make things right with me. Hell, I must have been out of my damn mind."

"Look, I don't want this divorce to turn into something ugly, because it doesn't have to be that way. We can split everything up so that neither one of us gets the low end of the deal."

"You know what," she said, standing up. "I want you to get your sorry ass out of here right now. Just looking at you makes me want to throw up. Get the fuck out," she screamed, walking into the kitchen. The devil had led her in there and was advising her to grab the first butcher knife she could get her hands on, but at the same time, she heard what must have been an angel begging her to let this whole thing go. She didn't know what to do.

"I'll have my attorney send you the divorce papers within the next couple of weeks," he said. He walked toward the front door and pulled it open.

Regina stormed out of the kitchen—fortunately, without any sharp weapons—and responded. "You can serve me with all the papers you want to, but I'm not signing a damn thing until I get good and ready. And you can forget about marrying Miss Marilyn before she delivers that baby of yours, because it ain't happenin', brother."

Larry walked out the door and slammed it.

She was more furious now than before. Who in the hell did he think he was anyway, ignoring her like she was some puppet? She swung open the door and rushed outside, onto the edge of the lawn by the driveway. "When I get through with you, you'll be wishing you'd never met me. And if you thought having a rock thrown through your car window was insane, well, just wait. When this is all over, you'll be on your knees begging me to take your sorry ass back. Except, it won't be happening."

He turned the ignition to the car and leaned out the window. "Whether you want to or not, you're going to have to get over me. I've got who I want, and like I told you before, you're just going to have to accept it. That's just the way it is. And as far as all your little threats, you're wasting your breath," he said, rolling out of the driveway.

She wanted to chase after him on foot, but since this was the neighborhood she *did* had to live in, she couldn't clown nearly as bad as she had over at Marilyn's on Monday. Her white neighbors would think she was some sort of a troublemaker, and it wouldn't be long before they would start classifying her as being "just like the rest." She couldn't have that. She wanted them to know that there was such a thing as decent black people. She went back inside the house and shut the door.

She dropped down on the oversized chair once again, stretched her feet out on the matching ottoman, and tried to keep up with all of the thoughts racing through her mind. Something wasn't right. Here, Larry had told her he was in love with some slut, was expecting a baby, and was filing for a divorce within a couple of weeks, and for some strange reason, she really didn't feel all that hurt. Sure, she was shocked, felt betrayed, and was angry as hell, but the feelings she was experiencing right at the moment weren't nearly as bad as when she'd busted them in Atlanta or when she'd realized he'd moved in with Marilyn. Maybe she was in denial. Or maybe she'd only wanted to get back together with him because she still wasn't crazy about the idea of being alone. She'd been asking God on a daily basis to give her the strength to get over Larry, and she wondered if that's what was happening. Maybe her prayers had been answered without her even paying much attention.

A part of her had wanted to get back together with Larry, but after seeing him and hearing his headline news, that idea was the furthest thing from her mind. She wouldn't have him now if he were the last bastard on this earth. How she could fall in and out of love, be hurt one moment and enjoying herself the next, was beyond her. She'd been on an emotional roller coaster ever since this crazy shit had started and couldn't wait for it to be over with.

She took a deep breath and looked at the glass-shelved grandfather clock. It was just past six. Sitting around the house on a Saturday night was the last thing she wanted to do, and she wasn't going to. Instead, she was going to spend the night out on the town and was taking Karen right along with her. They were both having marital problems and desperately needed a girls' night out, anyway.

She reached for the phone and hit the key for Karen's number, which was programmed in the memory feature. As she waited for Karen to answer, she thought, "Hmmph. If Larry thinks he's the only Negro with a dick between his legs, he's dead wrong—and after tonight, I'm going to be the one to prove it to him."

CHAPTER 17

"S HIT, WHEN WAS the last time we went out?" Regina asked Karen while entering I-90, heading east. It was half past ten o'clock, the traffic was fairly moderate, and they were still a few miles away from Le Club, which was located down in the Loop on Michigan Avenue.

"I don't know," Karen said. "But it had to have been at least a year ago. And even then, we were out with those no-good men we're married to. I'm so glad you called and said you wanted to go out. Shit, why should we sit at home all alone just because John and Larry are fucking up?"

"Damn," Regina said, laughing. "You've used that word more in the last couple of months than during the whole time I've known you. This gambling thing has brought the worst out in you, hasn't it?"

"Shit, you know how I am when it comes to money, and this thing with John is too much. I'm not having it, and he knows it. Just thinking about him makes me angry."

"I know I bring this up almost every time we talk, but I still say you should give him one more chance. I know you're upset about those withdrawals he made, but maybe he'll finally go to one of those meetings."

"But even if he does go, I still won't trust him. Whenever he's gone, I'll think he's at the track, and whenever he gets paid, I'll always want to know where every dime of his money goes. I'd be giving him the third degree whenever he's only a few minutes late coming home. What kind of life is that for me or him? Shit, that would be no different than suspecting that he was screwing around with some other woman."

"Girl, don't even go there, because I can tell you from personal experience that gambling and adultery are far from being the same. Shoot, the way I see it, you should be counting your blessings, because at least John isn't screwing around and having a baby by someone you once believed was your friend. If you ask me, that's the type of shit you divorce somebody over."

"Don't get me wrong, I do love John, but we can't make it without money. Before you know it, bill collectors will be calling the house, and I'm not about to have that. If I wanted to struggle to pay bills all by myself, I would have stayed single. Shit, I already divorced one irresponsible Negro, so you know it wouldn't be but a thing for me to do it again, if I had to."

"Please. You're just upset about what happened earlier. Tomorrow will be a different day, and I guarantee you'll think twice about divorcing him," Regina said, pulling out her Capri cigarettes and pressing down the lighter on the dashboard of the Mercedes. Shit, Karen was going to find out sooner or later, anyway.

Karen looked at her. "When did you start that back up?" she asked, already cracking her window.

"Girl, I've been smoking my ass off ever since I came back from Atlanta. I just didn't want you to know it. I thought I was going to die when we were at the mall yesterday. I didn't have one the whole time."

"As hard as it was for you to give it up, I can't believe you did that."

"Shoot, I just couldn't help it. My nerves were shot, and smoking a cigarette was the only thing that kind of calmed me down. It's a shame, I know, but there's nothing I can do about it now," Regina said, lighting her cigarette. As soon as she took the first puff, it dawned on her. The doctor had run tests for anemia earlier today, but that probably wasn't why she'd been dizzy at all. More than likely it was these cigarettes.

"You know, you sure are taking this pregnancy thing awfully well. If it were me, I think I'd be somewhere blowing somebody's head off," Karen said, thinking back on what Regina had told her when she'd phoned earlier in the evening.

"I just don't feel like that for some reason. I wanted to kill both of them when we were over at Marilyn's this week, but now I really don't care about either one of them. All I want to do is get on with my life. One month ago, I would have died to be with Larry and would have done anything for him, but now, I really couldn't care less. I still love him, but it's not the same as it used to be. Atlanta was one thing, moving in with her was another, but getting her pregnant was the icing on the cake. They can have each other, because I'm through with the whole thing."

"What are you going to do about the house?"

"Shit, I'm not hauling my butt anywhere until the divorce is final. Hell, why should I have to worry about finding somewhere to stay when he's the one that moved his ass out in the first place?"

"Yeah, but what about after the divorce is over?"

"Who knows? I'll probably rent a condo or something. But, I will say this, if he wants to keep the house, he's going to have to pay me a huge settlement, because I'll be damned if I'm going to let him move Marilyn's ass in there just like that. And the divorce isn't going to be as simple as he thinks, either. He's been so caught up with Marilyn that he never stopped one time to think about what the consequences would be if he moved out on me the way he did. That motherfucker thinks he's going to strut into some courtroom, divorce my ass, and live happily ever after, but when I counter his motion on the grounds of desertion, he's going to wake up real fast. He even had the nerve to forward his mail over to Marilyn's address. Any fool knows that the post office keeps a record of information like that. I mean, how stupid can one man be?"

Karen laughed. "Are you serious?"

"As a heart attack," Regina said, taking a drag from her Capri. "Men are so naive sometimes."

"It's either that, or they think we are. Shit, what they need to realize is that when they're sleeping, we're thinking. I used to do that all the time. When John was still at the house, he'd be snoring, and I'd be thinking a thousand thoughts."

"Something's wrong with them, and if you ask me, Eve should have been put on this earth first. She might've made the mistake of eating that apple, but I'm willing to bet she had more common sense in her baby finger than Adam had in his whole head."

They both laughed. Regina drove past the club and parked down the street. They checked their lipstick and powder to make sure everything was intact and stepped out of the car. It wasn't cold, but it wasn't as warm as it should be either, given that it was almost the end of May. Regina wore a sleeveless, closely fitted, brownish-colored dress, matching heels, and off-white panty hose. Karen wore a black sleeveless sweater and a black crepe skirt.

They walked up to the line that consisted of nine or ten people, mostly women, and looked at each other. Not much had changed since when they'd been single. There always seemed to be more women out than men. Of course, that didn't faze Karen, since she wasn't looking for a man to take home anyway, but Regina was having different thoughts. She was on a mission and wasn't planning to leave this place until she'd found the perfect one-night stand. She wasn't about to go one more evening without having an orgasm, and that was that. Karen would have thought she was crazy, with AIDS floating around the way it was, and that was the main reason she'd decided to keep her plans to herself. It was just better that way. No sense in upsetting the girl about something she'd already made her mind up about anyway.

They paid the ten-dollar cover charge and entered the club. It wasn't all that packed yet, but most people never seemed to come out until after eleven or so. They walked over to the first table they saw and took a seat.

"Everything still looks the same," Regina said, casing the place.

"Yeah, it sure does." Karen set her purse on the table. "It's still a nice place to go, though, when you want to get out of the house."

Shoot, Regina thought, that wasn't why she was there at all. It was true that she'd wanted to get out of the house, but her main reason for coming here was to find someone who wanted to have sex and who wasn't going to expect anything after the little escapade was over. "But where are all the men? I mean, I was expecting way more than this," Regina said without even thinking. Damn. Just that quickly she'd told off on herself. She couldn't keep shit from Karen no matter how hard she tried.

"I know you're not thinking about hooking up with

some brother that you don't know anything about, are you?"

Regina batted her eyes and grinned slyly. "I'm not saying anything."

"Please tell me you're not thinking about. . . ." Karen paused and gazed down at Regina's left ring finger. That rock Larry had given her for their engagement was missing, and so was her diamond-encrusted wedding band. "That's exactly what you're thinking about, aren't you? I don't believe you."

"What?" Regina said, still grinning.

Karen shook her head.

"I'm sorry, but I'm sick of being by myself. And anyway, wouldn't you rather see me trying to have a good time instead of sitting around the house moping like some stray puppy?"

"You know I would, but I just want you to be careful. There's too many diseases out here. All I'm saying is, if you do anything, please make sure the guy has a condom. Things have gotten worse since before we were married, and finding a safe sex partner is like playing Russian roulette."

"Girl, don't even worry about that. I would never do anything without protection."

"All right now. Just make sure you don't," Karen said, scanning the room. "Hey, isn't that the guy you purchased that tennis bracelet from yesterday?"

"Where?" Regina said, quickly turning her head in the same direction that Karen was looking in.

"Over there." Karen pointed as discreetly as possible. "The guy with the double-breasted suit on."

"That's definitely him," Regina said. "And looking finer than he did yesterday. Shit."

"You kind of like him, don't you?"

"It's been so long since I had to look at any guy in that way, I don't know if I do or not. And, although it probably sounds petty, I don't know if I even want to think about getting mixed up with someone who works as a salesclerk in some jewelry store."

"If the man is nice and will treat you right, you'd better get that out of your head. That asshole you're married to now makes a ton of money, and look how he turned out."

"You've definitely got a point there."

"Oh shit," Karen said, laughing under her voice. "Here he comes."

By then, there wasn't any time for Regina to respond.

"How's it going, ladies?" he asked, smiling, a drink in his hand.

"Fine," they both answered.

"I don't think I've ever seen either one of you in here before. Is this your first time?"

"No," Regina said. "We've been in here before, but not in a long time. You come here often?"

"Actually, I come quite a bit. At least a couple times a month."

Regina didn't know what else to say and felt as nervous as some schoolgirl talking for the first time to a boy she liked.

Karen picked up on it and spoke up. "You can have a seat if you want to. We're not expecting anyone else."

Regina looked at her in disbelief.

"If that's okay with both of you, I will," he said, directing the comment to Regina.

"It's okay with me," Regina said.

He sat down. "I guess the least I could do is introduce myself. I'm Malcolm Taylor." He shook Regina's hand and then Karen's.

"I'm Karen Jackson."

"I'm Regina Moore."

"Nice to meet both of you, although I guess we sort of already met indirectly at the jewelry store," he said, looking at Regina's wrist. "I see you've got the bracelet on, huh?"

"Sure do. It's really nice, and I'm glad I bought it."

Regina felt uncomfortable and couldn't understand it at first, but then it dawned on her. She was seriously attracted to the man. And he must have felt the same way about her, because he hadn't taken his eyes off her for more than two seconds ever since he'd approached the table. The chemistry between them was so thick that it was almost visible. This just couldn't be. She'd only been separated from her husband for two weeks, and here she was already attracted to another man. And to top it off, she could hardly see Malcolm as being the one-night stand she'd come there to look for. Gosh. She wasn't ready for anything like this. At least not yet.

"Can I buy you ladies a drink?" he asked.

"No, I'm fine," Karen said. "But thanks for asking."

"I'm fine for now, too," Regina added.

"I'm going to the ladies' room," Karen said. "I'll be right back, though." She rose and walked away from the table.

Damn. The last thing Regina wanted was to be left alone with this gorgeous man. Oh, she wasn't the slightest bit worried about what he might do; it was herself she didn't trust. She couldn't believe Karen had left and not asked her to go with her the way she usually did whenever they were out somewhere, and it was obvious that she'd done it on purpose. She'd have to deal with Karen later.

Malcolm swallowed the last of his drink. "You wanna dance?"

"Sure."

By the time they made their way across the dance floor, some fast song Regina didn't recognize had finished playing, and the beginning notes of "Before I Let You Go" by Blackstreet had already started. Of course, it had to be a slow one, she thought.

Malcolm pulled her as close to him as was publicly appropriate, wrapped his arms around her waist, and waited for her to position her hands on his shoulders. They started two-stepping. She couldn't believe how wonderful it felt to lean against this man she'd hardly known for less than an hour. It felt like she'd known him for years. She'd been attracted to Larry from the very beginning when she'd first met him, too, but it hadn't been anything like this. The sensations pulsating through her body were almost too much for her to handle. Her heart was pounding hard, and it felt like it was going to explode.

He looked down at her. "So, tell me. What man in his right mind would allow his beautiful wife to go out on a Saturday night to a club filled with a bunch of single men?"

Shoot. She'd left her wedding rings at home in her jewelry case, and she wondered how he could possibly know she was married. "How did you know I had a husband?"

"Because yesterday you had on a set of wedding rings and the credit card you used had the name Larry Moore on it. That was a dead giveaway."

She'd forgotten all about that. She chuckled quietly and said, "Do you always memorize the names on every credit card you see?"

"No, actually I don't. But there was something special about you, and I couldn't help but remember the name."

"Oh, really?"

"Yes. Really."

"Well, to make a long story short, we're about to go through a divorce, so I guess you could say I'm married, but not for long."

"I'm sorry things didn't work out for you. It's never an easy thing when two people have to break up."

Regina didn't say anything, but she wondered if maybe he'd gone through a divorce himself, since it sounded like he understood what she was experiencing.

"It really feels good, holding you like this," he said.

Regina didn't know if she was ready for such straight-forwardness and decided not to respond.

"I didn't say anything out of line, did I?" he asked.

"No. Why'd you think that?"

"Because you're not saying anything."

Hmmph. Actually, she had a lot to say, but she wasn't about to let him know it. He felt good to her too, and to be honest, she wished the dance would never end. That she could lie in his arms from now until the end of time. "No. You didn't say anything out of line."

"Good. Because the last thing I want to do is upset you."

Regina glanced over at their table and caught Karen's eye. They smiled at each other. Regina had been so caught up in her conversation with Malcolm that she hadn't even noticed Karen returning from the ladies' room. She couldn't wait to tell her how attracted she was to Malcolm and how comfortable she felt with him. It was almost too good to be true. And although she hated to think about it, she wondered if it was.

When the song ended, TLC's "Red Light Special" began with no break in between. Regina and Malcolm kept slow dancing.

KAREN LOOKED AWAY from the dance floor and saw a petite-sized waitress approaching her.

"Can I get you anything?" the waitress asked.

Karen was already starting to get bored and decided

that maybe if she had a drink, things might liven up a bit. "Sure. I'll have a citrus wine cooler. Whatever brand you have is fine." Karen never usually drank, so the label on the beverage really didn't matter to her.

When the waitress walked away, Karen scanned the room again. This place wasn't nearly as exciting as she'd thought it would be. And although she dreaded admitting it, it wasn't the same without John. Damn him for ruining their marriage.

As the waitress set the drink down on the table, Karen pulled money out of her purse and paid her. But when the waitress started to walk away again, she sensed someone standing behind her, and she turned around. It was John.

He pulled around the chair Regina had been sitting in and sat down. "Hey, we need to talk, and I'm not taking no for an answer."

Karen was shocked to see him and couldn't believe how pushy he was acting. This wasn't his way of handling things, and she wondered what had gotten into him.

"How'd you know where I was?"

"That's not important," John said, pulling her up from the table by her wrist.

Karen jerked her arm away from him. "I just know you're not trying to strong-arm me. You must be out of your damn mind, because I'm not going anywhere with you."

"Hey, I didn't mean to grab you like that, but we really do need to talk."

"What I want to know is how you knew where I was. What have you been doing? Spying on me?"

"Damn it, Karen. What difference does it make?"

"It makes a lot of difference to me."

"I called Regina to talk to her about us, and she told me you were coming down here. Now, are you satisfied?"

"Regina had no right doing that, and you had no right calling her."

"She's your best friend. You've never had a problem with me talking to Regina before, so what's the problem now?"

"Oh, don't get me wrong. I have no problem with you talking to her, I just don't want you guys scheming behind my back," Karen said, staring straight at Regina, who was smiling. Karen furnished her with a dirty look and glanced in another direction.

"Karen, please. You know good and well we weren't scheming behind your back. Why don't you stop acting like this and just come outside with me."

Karen was getting pissed off, and since she didn't want to show her ass in front of a bunch of strangers, she figured it was best to go outside like John wanted. They strolled a ways down the street until they were alone.

"Look," Karen said. "I've given you chance after chance to correct your shit, but you've refused to do it. You knew what the consequences were, but you kept doing what you were doing, anyway. You made your bed and now you have to lie in it. It's as simple as that."

"I haven't gone to the track since the day I made that

last withdrawal, which was over a week and a half ago. I knew it was wrong, and I haven't done anything like that since. I went too far that time, and I'm aware of it. I told you I was going to go to one of those meetings tomorrow, and I meant it. I'm not here to beg you, but I'll be damned if I'm going to let you end things between us without getting a chance to explain myself."

"I don't see what you have to explain. You've thrown a ton of money away, and as far as I'm concerned, that sums up everything. You have a problem, and when a person has a problem, they do whatever it takes to remedy the situation."

"It's not that easy. You don't understand, because you don't have any unusual problems or an obsessive personality like I do. When I gave up cigarettes, I became addicted to caffeine. Do you realize I drink at least six to seven cups of coffee every day? When I saw that the lottery wasn't paying off, I started going to the track. Whenever I give up one obsession I search and search until I find some other outlet. It's not about becoming rich from betting on the horses, it's about being obsessed with winning. It gives me a sense of satisfaction that I can't even explain. It's almost like getting high. Like I'm living on the edge. I can't explain why I do it, but when I'm inside Arlington and I'm waiting for those horses to race around that track, I get a feeling like I've never felt before. And as much as I hate to say it, not even you can give me that. It's a sickness, and I know that now."

Karen couldn't believe what she was hearing. It was as

though he was finally reaching out to her. He'd never confessed his feelings like this before, and she wasn't sure how she should respond. She waited for him to continue.

"Baby, please. Just wait for me. I know after what you found out today you're probably wanting to divorce me, but I'm asking you to give me some time to get myself together. Once I get more involved with Gamblers Anonymous, I know things will be different. I wish I could have started way before now, but I just couldn't see it. I mean, I knew I had a problem, but I honestly believed I could handle it. And if it makes any difference to you, I didn't blow the entire fifteen hundred dollars. I used the money from that second withdrawal to get the transmission on the Beamer repaired."

She couldn't believe it. He'd actually done something logical with part of the money he'd taken from the account. This was good news, and it made her feel just a little better about all of this.

"I love you more than anything," she finally said. "But I can't live my life like this anymore. The last thing I ever wanted to do was be separated from you, but at the time, I didn't see any other way," she said, holding back what was sure to be huge crocodile tears if she released them.

John took her in his arms. "I love you, baby, and I'll be damned if I'm going to let gambling cause our marriage to break up," he said, sniffling.

Was he crying? She couldn't remember if he'd ever done that in front of her before. Maybe when someone had died, but never over something like this. She hugged him tight, and for the first time in a while, she could tell she was doing the right thing. He'd taken $1,500 from their accounts, and there was no way she could merely pretend it hadn't happened, but she was willing to stand by his side as long as he attended those meetings religiously.

Her mother had been advising her over and over again to work with John on his problem, but she'd never taken her seriously, until now. As far as Karen had been concerned, this was John's problem, and it was up to him to be a man and take care of it. But now she had to admit that maybe that hadn't been the right attitude, especially since she had a certain responsibility when it came to their marriage, the same as he did. She'd promised to stay with him in sickness and in health, for richer or for poorer, for better or worse, and it was time she acted like it.

"Hey," John said, grabbing both sides of her face with his hands and gazing straight into her eyes. "Don't be mad at Regina. She was only doing what she thought was right. She doesn't want to see us apart, and that's why she tried to get us together tonight."

"Yeah. I know. I'd better go back in there so I can apologize for looking at her the way I did. She probably thinks I'm a real bitch."

They walked back down to the club and went inside.

"Why don't you tell her that you're going to leave with me," John said.

Karen looked at him indecisively, because she wasn't sure if she should leave with him or not. On the one hand, she couldn't wait to spend the night with him, but on the other, she was scared shitless that he might not hold up his end of the deal by going to that meeting tomorrow. She decided to take her chances, though. "Are you ready now, or do you want to stay a while longer?" Karen asked.

"I'm ready whenever you are."

Karen beckoned for Regina to meet her halfway across the room.

"You know you really pushed it this time, don't you?" Karen asked, smiling.

"Girl, please. I knew you would have been upset if you'd known what I was up to, but I just couldn't stand the thought of you and John not being together. It didn't make any sense."

"Well, we had a long talk, and I think things are about to fall back into place with us, so I guess instead of being mad at you for sticking your nose into our business, I should be thanking you. Actually, the best thing you could have done was bring me here, because it didn't take more than a few minutes for me to look around and realize that I definitely don't want to go back to the dating scene, and I definitely don't want to give up a man who loves me the way John does."

Regina laughed. "I'm glad you finally came to your senses. With your stubborn self."

Karen rolled her eyes and laughed. "John and I are getting ready to leave, so I wanted to come let you know," Karen said, glancing over at Malcolm. "And from what I can see, three's a crowd, anyway. It doesn't look like you need me at all."

"Girl, please. I'll have to call you tomorrow and fill you in, but the one thing I can tell you right now, is that he's got it going on. And I feel like I've known him my entire life. He's such a sweetheart. I could sit and talk with him all night and still have a shitload of conversation left over. Oh, and guess what? You won't believe this. Remember how skeptical I was about him being a salesclerk?"

"Uh-huh."

"Well, a few minutes ago, he told me that he owns the jewelry store we were in and three others located in the surrounding area. The only reason he was working yesterday was that his manager all of a sudden quit, and he hasn't had a chance to hire a new one. Can you believe that? I mean, shoot."

"I guess you never know, do you? But actually we should have known something was up when we saw how sharp he was dressed yesterday, not to mention that suit he's got on right now. No salesclerk could afford that type of clothing."

"That's for sure. Well, I better get back over to the table, because Malcolm is the last person I want to keep waiting."

"Don't forget to call me tomorrow when you wake up. That is, if you're alone," Karen said and laughed.

"Girl, shut up. It's not even like that. At least not yet, anyway. You and John have a good time," Regina said, hugging Karen.

"We will. I love you, and thanks again for doing what you did for John and me. You have no idea how much it means."

CHAPTER 18

AFTER ARRIVING HOME from the club the previous night, Karen and John had laughed, reminisced, and made love until sometime after three in the morning. It was now ten o'clock. Karen was lying across the bed on her stomach listening to Pam, the gospel music DJ for V103, and John was in the shower.

He'd phoned his mother just before getting out of bed, letting her know that he was moving back home and that he'd be at her place around noon to move his things. Something he probably wished he hadn't done, since the woman had thrown the pissiest fit of all times. Karen had actually heard her screaming at him through the phone. She'd sounded like some woman who'd just recently discovered that her husband was leaving her for another woman. And to Karen, that was about the craziest shit she'd ever heard of. Hell, she was his mother, not his wife. If she'd said it once, she'd said it a thousand times: The woman needed to get a life. Needed someone to rock her little world. To put it plainly, she needed something she obviously hadn't had in a very long time: hot, buck-wild sex.

Karen felt guilty for having such devilish thoughts like that on a Sunday morning, but the woman always seemed to bring out the worst in her. It had always been that way, and as far as she could see, it was never going to change.

As she rolled over on her back, the phone rang. It rang a second time before she finally picked it up. "Hello?"

"Hi, Auntie Karen," her niece whispered. "It's me. Shaniqua."

Karen couldn't remember one time when Shaniqua had ever sounded like she was sneaking to make a phone call to her. Something had to be wrong. "Hi, sweetheart. How are you?"

"I'm fine."

"What are you doing calling me this early on a Sunday morning, little girl?" Karen tried to sound cheerful and unworried.

"My mommy is pregnant again," Shaniqua said without delay and in a lower tone of voice than before.

A wave of nervousness and frustration flashed through Karen's body, and her eyes were already filling with water. "Maybe you heard her wrong, sweetheart."

"No. I didn't, Auntie Karen. She and Daddy were arguing about it last night."

Karen had warned Sheila at least a hundred times about having adult conversations in front of those children, and still the girl hadn't stopped doing it. She was afraid to even ask what else Shaniqua had heard, but she went ahead anyway. "Why were they arguing?"

"Because my daddy doesn't want my mommy to have any more babies, and he wants her to have an abortion. What's an abortion, Auntie Karen?"

Dear God. That was why the poor little thing had called. She'd probably been awake most of the night trying her hardest to figure out what an abortion was. Karen didn't have the slightest idea as to how she was supposed to answer her niece's question. She didn't have any kids, and until now, she'd never had to worry about anything like this. "It's really a grown-folks' word and something you should talk to your mom about."

Shaniqua was quiet.

Karen figured she'd better say something. "Don't think you did anything wrong by asking me about it, because you didn't. It's just that I think it'll be better if your mom explains it to you. I'll call and talk to her about it later. Now, are you going to be all right?"

"Uh-huh," Shaniqua said, sounding sweet, innocent, and slightly confused.

"We'd better hang up now, so the phone bill won't be so high. Okay?"

"Okay."

"I love you, honey."

"I love you too, Auntie Karen."

As soon as Karen laid the phone on the hook, tears flowed down her face. Why was this happening? And what in the world was Sheila going to do with a fourth mouth to feed? She was having a hard enough time trying to feed the three she already had. If only she'd had her tubes tied, like Karen had suggested. Couldn't Sheila see that she was making things harder not just for herself but for her children as well?

John stepped out of the bathroom with a towel gathered around his waist and saw that Karen's face was wet. "What's the matter, baby?" he asked, moving closer to her. He sat down on the bed and hugged her as tightly as he could. "What's wrong?"

Karen sniffled a couple of times, swallowed, and took a deep breath. "Sheila's pregnant again."

"What? Baby, I'm so sorry," he said, rubbing her back. "What is she going to do?"

"I don't know, but Shaniqua says she heard Terrance trying to talk her into having an abortion."

"What does Shaniqua know about having an abortion?"

"She doesn't, and I'm pretty sure that's why she called me."

"I don't know what to say, baby. I thought your sister knew better than to let something like this happen again."

"Yeah, I did too, or at least that's what I'd been hoping."

"Does your mother know yet?"

"I doubt it. I guess I better call her now. I hate to even

tell her, because she's been saying all along that something like this was going to happen."

"Are you going to be okay?"

"I'll be fine. Go on and finish getting dressed."

He kissed her on the forehead and went back into the bathroom.

She picked up the phone again and dialed her mother's number.

"Hello?" Lucinda answered.

"Hi, Mom," Karen said, trying to sound upbeat. "How are you?"

"Fine. How are you?"

"Everything's good. John and I have worked things out, and he's moving his things back home this afternoon."

"I'm so glad to hear that. I've got some good news for you, too."

Lucinda was sounding so happy that Karen knew it had to be something big. "What's going on?"

"Well, you know Richard has been pressing me about marriage, but I've been putting him off."

"Yeah. And?"

"I told him last night that I was finally ready."

"Oh, Mom, that's great. I have no doubt that you're making the right decision. He's a good man."

"Yes, he is. It's a big step, and it's kind of scary, but I decided that I don't want to mess around and lose somebody that treats me as well as he does."

"So, when is the big day?"

"Probably sometime in August. It'll be a small ceremony, but I will need you to be my matron of honor."

"You know that's not a problem. We'll have to sit down next weekend and start planning the reception."

"Well, I don't want to rush you off the phone, but I'd better get back to doing my makeup before Richard gets here. We're going to church."

"Okay. I'll talk to you later on tonight."

"Bye," Lucinda said and hung up.

Karen shook her head. She'd wanted desperately to tell her mother about Sheila, but she just couldn't bring herself to say anything that was going to ruin one of the best days of her mother's life. It was better to wait and break the news to her tomorrow.

CHAPTER 19

REGINA SET DOWN the bowl of potato salad that she'd made early this morning and hugged Karen. It was Sunday, two days before Independence Day, and Karen had invited her over for a pre-Fourth of July cook-out. Since they both usually spent all of the holidays with their own families, it had always been a tradition for the four of them to get together a day or two before—Karen, Regina, John, and Larry. Except this time, Larry wasn't part of the get-together, Malcolm was.

"How's it going, girl?" Regina asked, smiling.

"Fine. I would ask how things are with you, but from that huge smile on your face, it's obvious. You're glowing like a lightbulb."

They both laughed.

"Girl, Malcolm and I have only been seeing each other for about six weeks, but we've grown so close to each other. Shoot, I think I'm in love with the man," Regina said, setting her miniature red purse on the kitchen counter. She was wearing an ankle-length, solid-red knit dress.

"I kind of thought you were. I'm really happy for you, because you deserve someone like Malcolm. Where is he, anyway?"

"He's bringing in the pop that you wanted me to pick up. I think John's out there helping him."

"Thanks for picking that up for me. I can't believe I remembered to get everything except something to drink. Especially since it seems like we do more drinking than eating," Karen said, fixing the collar of her white, sleeveless, mock turtleneck shirt. She wore black, cuffed shorts to go with it.

"No problem. The store was right on the way over here. Do you need me to help you with anything?"

"I think I've got everything under control. John cooked the spaghetti, and he's grilling the meat now. The only thing I did was arrange the items that don't require any cooking."

Regina laughed. "You are so crazy. What kind of meat is John grilling?"

"Cornish hens, ribs, pork chops, and brats. He's just about done, though."

"Shoot, who did he think was coming over, the entire suburb? Who's going to eat all of that?"

"John. He won't eat a whole lot when we sit down for dinner, but he'll trace back and forth from the TV to the kitchen all night long. And since he doesn't have to work tomorrow, he probably won't go to bed until around two or three in the morning, after he finishes watching those pay channels. He never gains any weight, but he can really put away a lot of food."

"I guess so," Regina said, pulling the refrigerator door open. "What else did you get?"

Karen took a half dozen dinner rolls out of a plastic bag and placed them single file on a baking sheet, laced each of them with margarine, and stuck them in the oven. "Macaroni salad, Italian salad, fruit salad, and chocolate ice cream for dessert."

"Hey, Karen," Malcolm said, walking into the room wearing a taupe pullover and a pair of matching shorts. As usual he was dressed sharp.

Both Karen and Regina turned to look at him.

"I'm good. How are you, Malcolm?" Karen reached out to hug him.

"I'm doing fine, as long as I'm with my baby," he said, kissing Regina.

"I heard that," Karen said, smiling.

Regina blushed from ear to ear.

John entered next, dressed in a pair of tan linen shorts and a white polo shirt. Like Malcolm, he was looking casually sharp, but then for John, that was commonplace. "What's going on, Regina?" he said, hugging her.

"Not much, John. What's up with you?"

"What do you mean not much," John asked raising his eyebrows. "From the look on your face, it seems to me like a whole lot is going on."

"Shut up, John." Regina punched him in his shoulder. They all laughed.

Karen looked around the kitchen. "I thought you guys were bringing in the pop?"

"We put them on the patio, so we could throw them in the cooler," John said, opening the top half of the refrigerator. He pulled out two large plastic bags of ice and passed one of them to Malcolm.

"The meat should be done in about twenty minutes or so," John said, brushing past Karen and stealing a feel from her butt. "You can go ahead and start bringing out the rest of the food, if you want to."

"You think you're slick, don't you?" Karen asked him.

"Shit. I am," he said, winking and grinning at Karen.

Regina and Malcolm laughed.

After the men went back onto the patio, Regina grabbed the left side of her chest and pretended she could physically feel her heart. "Oooh, girl. I get a chill every time Malcolm comes anywhere near me."

"I can tell. I don't think you were this caught up when you met Larry. At least it doesn't seem like you were," Karen said, removing the rolls from the oven.

"I wasn't. Malcolm is so gentle with me. He's polite, and he knows how to treat me. I've never met a man who was so concerned with what I want and how I feel. Larry was a good provider, but when it came to feelings, all he cared about was himself. I almost can't believe I was ever in love with him. And worse than that, I can't believe I'm falling for someone else so quickly. I mean, Larry and I have only been split up for about two and a half months. I sometimes wonder if we ever had real love in the first place, and I'm starting to think that maybe it was his looks and paychecks that I was so attracted to, and not him as a person at all."

"Well, whatever the reason, at least you won't have to deal with him much longer. When is the divorce going to be finalized, anyway?"

"Probably in a few months," Regina said and took a seat at the table. "I wish it could be a lot sooner, but when property is involved, the process takes a lot longer than usual."

"Just be thankful you don't have any children that you have to worry about. Have you heard from him?" Karen asked while removing plastic silverware, paper plates, and matching napkins from the cupboard above the sink.

"As a matter of fact, I heard from him last night. He called me saying he needed to discuss something with me and that it had to do with the divorce. He wanted to come over this morning, but when I told him I had plans, he said he was going to drop by Wednesday evening after I get home from work."

"What do you think he wants to talk about?"

"Who knows. We haven't spoken more than a couple times since he had me served with the divorce papers, so I don't know what's up. Knowing Larry, though, it has something to do with the settlement."

"I wouldn't budge on anything if I were you. To tell you the truth, I don't even know if I would let him come over."

"I know, but since things have been pretty civil between us, I don't see how it could hurt anything."

"Does he know that you're seeing someone?"

"No. And that's how I plan on keeping it until the judge signs that divorce decree. The last thing I want to do is give him any ammunition to use against me in court. And I sure as hell don't want him to know that I've been thinking about moving in with Malcolm."

"You didn't tell me that," Karen said in amazement.

"I wasn't sure how you were going to react. You know how conservative you are."

"Well, I don't have a problem with it, and neither should Larry, if you ask me. Shit, he's living with a woman who's carrying his baby, and that's ten times worse than what you're planning to do. At least you're going to wait until the divorce is final before you make your move. Hell. He couldn't even do that."

"I know. But I'm not taking any chances. Plus, I don't want any conflicts between the two of them. Larry has who he wants, but I doubt very seriously if he'd be jumping up and down at the fact that I'm in love with someone else. You know how men are. They might not want you, but they sure as hell don't want anyone else to have you either."

"Does Malcolm know you're letting him come over?"

"I told him all about it on the way over here, and he says he understands."

"Well, at least you don't have to worry about that. Hey, can you grab those salads out of the fridge?" Karen asked

Regina. "That way we can start taking them out to the patio."

"Sure." Regina rose from the chair she was sitting in. "So enough about me. What about you and John?"

"Things couldn't be better. If anything, our marriage is better now than it was before. It's almost like our souls are closer. Like we understand each other a lot more. It's so easy to become self-satisfied when everything is going your way, and that's exactly what I was doing with John. I was happy with him so long as things were going the way I wanted them to, and not once did I ever consider how he might be feeling. For me, everything was great. We loved each other, trusted each other, had fun together, and for the most part, we were financially sound. But for John the picture was totally different. He was starting to feel down and out, and to make a long story short, it has a lot to do with his childhood. His father was a tyrant and was very violent. He pretty much ruined all of John's self-esteem, and that's why he has such an obsessive personality. That's why he always buys the best of everything, regardless of how much it costs. It makes him feel good, even though he knows the feeling is only temporary. And whenever his horses came in at the track, it made him feel like he'd really won big, and like he'd really accomplished something."

"Now, that's deep."

"Yeah, I know. All I can say is, thank God for Gamblers Anonymous, because without it, I don't know if our relationship would have survived. I mean, it's even helped me the couple of times I've gone with him. But also, I should be thanking you a thousand more times for asking him to come to the club that night. There's no telling if we would have ever gotten things back on track if you hadn't," Karen said, heading toward the patio with two pans in her hand.

"I owe you too," Regina said, following behind her. "I was feeling mighty low that Friday you came and picked me up to go shopping, and it was only after that did I start to see that I could make it without Larry if I had to. And Lord knows, I probably wouldn't have met Malcolm, since he rarely visits his stores on Fridays. Not to mention the fact that we usually go shopping on Saturdays. And the other thing is that I guess I sort of know how John feels because now that I'm happy with Malcolm, I don't feel the same need to shop as much as I used to."

"Girl, what would we do without each other?" Karen asked with tears in her eyes.

"That's just it," Regina said, smiling. "We wouldn't."

CHAPTER 20

REGINA HEARD the doorbell ringing, and went down the stairs. Larry had phoned earlier to say that he'd be over to talk to her around seven o'clock. All day, she'd felt sort of uneasy about this mystery meeting and couldn't wait for it to be over with.

He rang the doorbell again.

"Coming," she yelled as she approached the front door and pulled it open.

He walked in, proceeded through to the family room, and fell back on the love seat like he still lived there. She followed behind him and leaned her butt against the arm of the sofa. Two months ago, when she'd let him in to talk, he'd dropped that pregnancy newsflash on her. She couldn't wait to hear what he had to say this time.

"So how's everything been going?" he asked without taking one eye off her.

Regina wondered why he was staring at her the way he was. "Just fine," she said in a confident manner. "And you?"

He took a deep breath. "Actually, I'm not doing too well."

"Why is that? I'm giving you a divorce like you wanted, and you've got a baby on the way. So, I don't know how anything could possibly be wrong," she said sarcastically.

"I know you're going to be pissed off, but I have to say this."

"You have to say what?" Her curiosity was starting to get the best of her.

"I think we're making a big mistake by getting a divorce."

Regina cracked up laughing. "You've got to be kidding."

"I'm not kidding at all. We need to rethink this before it's too late. This whole thing is all wrong."

"Larry. Let's cut the bull, okay. What is this all about?"

"I want you back. I don't want a divorce. I don't know how I could have been so stupid," he said, pressing both his palms across the front of his face.

Was he crazy? Must've been, if he thought he could waltz his cheating ass in there and pick up where they'd left off before he'd started screwing around with Marilyn. "You told me that you were in love with Marilyn, that you were having a baby by her, and that you wanted a divorce. And if my memory serves me right, you told me that I was going to have to accept it, and that I was going to have to get over you. Remember?"

"I know what I said, but it was all a mistake. I wasn't thinking clearly. I don't love Marilyn, and we're not having any baby."

Damn. This fool was just full of surprises. "What do you mean you're not having a baby?"

"Just what I said. We're not having a baby."

The conversation was becoming more and more interesting by the minute, and she wished Karen was here to witness every bit of it. That way they could both laugh at his ass together. "So, what happened?"

Larry paused. "She had an abortion."

"She what?"

"She had an abortion a couple of weeks ago."

Now it all added up. Marilyn had ended her pregnancy and was dumping his two-timing ass. Regina couldn't believe any of what she was hearing. "So, what does having an abortion have to do with anything? If you love her the way you've been claiming, I don't see what the problem is."

"I'm not in love with her. And to tell you the truth, I don't know if I ever was."

"Then why in the hell did you keep saying you were? You kept throwing that shit in my face every single time I tried to talk to you."

"I guess I thought that I really did love her. But now I'm starting to see that it was nothing more than infatuation. Things weren't right between you and me, and I sort of lost it. If I had it to do all over again, I would never mess around on you. Not with Marilyn or anyone else. You've got to believe that, baby," he said, easing over to the sofa.

"Shit. I do believe you. No asshole ever misses his water until his well runs dry. That's been proven time and time again. You must think I'm just as loony as you are, though, because I know you don't expect me to believe that you're telling me the whole story. So, come on, Larry. Tell me what really happened between you and Marilyn? No. Don't even waste your breath answering that question. I'll do it for you. Marilyn saw you for the bastard that you really are, thought about it, went behind your back and had an abortion, and then dumped your sorry ass. And now, you think there's still time to get back with me. Am I right?"

He kneeled down directly in front of her and grabbed both of her hands in his. This was ridiculous, but at the same time, it was funny as hell. She'd told him how he was going to get down on his knees and beg her to take him back, and here he was, plain as day. Shit, maybe she should've become a psychic instead of an HR manager.

"No," he said. "It's not even like that. I'm here because I love you. Can't you see that?"

"Get your ass from in front of me," she said, shoving him and walking away. "You make me sick. When you brought your ass over here the last time, I would have gladly taken you back. It would have taken me a long time to get over what you did to me, but still, I would have taken you back. But like they say. That was then, and this is now. And now, it's too damn late for you. So, you might as well saddle up that horse you came in here on and ride your stupid ass on out of here, because ain't shit going on with you and me ever again."

Larry looked at her in a deranged way. Like he didn't know whether he was coming or going. "Why are you doing this, Regina? I told you I was sorry, and that I would make it up to you."

He was making her awfully tired, and her patience was drawing thinner by the second. "It's over between us, Larry. It took me a while, but I finally took your advice: I got over your ass. Now, you're the one who's going to have to accept it and get on with your life."

"Please, baby. Please don't do this," he said. Tears were rushing down his face.

Regina walked over to the front door, opened it, placed her left hand on her hip, and pursed her lips together. "Get out."

Larry kneeled on the floor for a few more minutes and then finally stood up. He dragged both his feet over to where Regina was standing and reached both of his hands out to her like he expected her to hug him. "Regina, I'm begging you. Don't do this."

Maybe he hadn't understood her when she'd told him to leave, but this time she was going to make sure that he did. She spoke slow and clear, but in a loud manner. "Get . . . the . . . hell . . . out!"

He left in silence, and she slammed the door as hard as

she could behind him. She leaned her back against the door, closed her eyes, and took a deep breath. She felt proud. Proud of the fact that she'd gone on with her life, gotten over Larry, and fallen in love with a wonderful man named Malcolm.

Just as she opened her eyes, the phone rang. She walked over to it and smiled when she saw Malcolm's number flash across the Caller ID screen. "Hello?" she said.

"Hey, sweetheart," he said.

"Hi, baby."

"So, is your company gone yet?"

"Actually, he just left."

"Are you okay?"

"Yeah, I'm fine."

"So, tell me," he said, sounding as if he was worried and unsure about something. "Is it just you and me now?"

Regina smiled and said, "Yes. It's definitely just you and me."

Here's a sneak preview of

TOO MUCH OF A GOOD THING

by Kimberla Lawson Roby

Available in hardcover
from William Morrow
An Imprint of HarperCollins*Publishers*

CURTIS RAISED the volume on his big-screen TV, slouched farther into the sofa, and sighed with much frustration. He hadn't slept peacefully in weeks. But he knew it was all because he'd been tossing and turning, night after night, trying desperately to dismiss the voice he kept hearing. It was a voice that demanded his return to the ministry.

For four long years he'd been trying to appreciate the fifty-thousand-dollar salary he earned as director of a delinquent teens facility, but it just wasn't working. It wasn't working because during his pastoral reign at Faith Missionary Baptist Church, he'd become completely accustomed to earning three times more than that—not to mention the thousands of dollars he received in love offerings. He could still remember how most of the members had worshipped the ground he walked on and how loads of women in the church had openly thrown themselves at his mercy. He'd tried to fight them off as best he could, but it wasn't long before he'd given in to Adrienne Jackson, the wife of one of the deacons. Then there was Charlotte, who was all of seventeen when he'd first begun seeing her and only eighteen when she gave birth to his illegitimate son. But he regretted nothing the way he regretted being caught on videotape having sex with two women he didn't know. He'd met them at a convenience store and taken them straight to a hotel, but what he hadn't counted on was their setting him up to be blackmailed. Monique, his disgruntled church secretary, had masterminded the entire scheme, and Curtis had lost everything: his tax-free six-figure income, three-thousand-plus congregation, custom-built dream house, and, most importantly, his wife and daughter to another man.

Curtis cringed at his latest thought, and then returned his attention to BET's morning inspiration segment. A world-renowned TV evangelist danced across the pulpit. Curtis had watched four others do the same thing every hour on the hour, and wished he could trade places with any one of them. He watched one massive audience after another rising to their feet, clapping, screaming, and giving high praises to God and the minister who was speaking before them. He watched so intensely that he was now drunk from all the excitement. These people on television reminded him of his own flock, the one he used to have, and he missed having them praise him in the same fashion. He missed the emotional high he always felt whenever he stood before his loyal congregation.

He continued watching the program and envied the evangelist, who wore the same type of suit he'd once worn himself. It had been a long while since he was able to buy anything that cost a thousand dollars, but that was finally about to change. He'd recently been approached by the deacon board of Truth Missionary Baptist Church. Truth was a church that had been founded by approximately one thousand of his former members, right after he was ousted. They were members who either hadn't believed the rumors they'd heard about him or who merely felt that he deserved to be forgiven the same as anyone else. They'd approached him about being their leader back then, too, but he'd declined when he decided that he no longer wanted to preach. Now, though, their charter pastor had left and taken a position at a church in D.C., and they needed to replace him.

For two weeks Curtis had debated whether he should accept their more than appealing offer, but in all honesty, he really didn't know how he could pass on it. They were offering him five thousand per week, his choice of any luxury vehicle, and a very respectable housing allowance—something he hadn't been able to negotiate at his previous church because they'd wanted him to live in some modest church parsonage. They were even willing to overlook the fact that he wasn't married as long as he found a wife within the first two years of his contract.

But Curtis didn't see a reason to wait that long and was sure that Mariah Johnson, the woman he'd been seeing for the past six months, would jump at the chance to marry him. As a matter of fact, she'd be perfect, because, unlike his ex-wife, Tanya, she knew her place. She was meek, mild, a bit naive, and completely submissive. She was beautiful but didn't know it, and the fact that she honored God and always tried to do the right thing wasn't going to hurt.

Curtis thought about all the rewards he was going to reap and wondered why he was still somewhat hesitant. But deep down he knew what it was. It was his mother and the scripture she had quoted him over and over, whenever he spoke about his desire to be filthy rich. She quoted Mark 8:36: "For what shall it profit a man, if he shall gain the whole world, and lose his own soul?"

But the more Curtis thought about it, the more he realized that Mark 8:36 really didn't apply to him. It didn't apply because he had no desire to gain the whole world.

He only wanted a very small part of it.

The part that rightfully belonged to him.

A Year Later

MARIAH JOHNSON BLACK smiled proudly as her husband neared the end of his morning message. It just didn't seem real, him actually being senior pastor of Truth Missionary Baptist Church or that he'd chosen her to be his wife. It didn't seem real that he'd wanted a woman who'd grown up in a run-down two-bedroom apartment on the West Side of Chicago that also housed her single mother and five siblings. But he always reminded her that he'd grown up with nothing himself. Still, every now and then, she had to pinch herself, because she couldn't believe how happy she was. She couldn't believe they'd only been married six short months, and yet Curtis had already bought her a six-thousand-square-foot house in Covington Park, the most expensive Mercedes that Daimler manufactured, and best of all, she didn't have to work for anyone. All she had to do was be the best wife she could be to Curtis and the best first lady to their congregation—two things Curtis said his first wife, Tanya, wasn't capable of. Mariah almost felt sorry for Tanya, because she couldn't imagine how painful it must have been, once Tanya realized what she'd given up. Curtis had told Mariah about Tanya's affair with James, and Mariah couldn't understand how Tanya even considered being with another man. Especially when she had someone as fine-looking and considerate as Curtis. Especially since he had only been with another woman—Adrienne—on two separate occasions. Curtis had told Mariah how he'd apologized and tried to explain everything to Tanya, but that she wasn't willing to forgive him. He'd tried to make Tanya see that this random act of adultery had only occurred because Satan was trying to attack him and their marriage. He'd told Tanya that the only reason God had allowed it to happen was because He wanted to see how strong their faith was and how committed they were to each other as husband and wife.

But thankfully, all of that was behind them now, and while she wasn't happy about Curtis and Tanya's marriage ending in divorce, she knew it was the only reason she was now sitting on the second pew, dressed in a royal blue suit, a matching hat, matching purse, and matching three-inch heels. Mariah also knew that Curtis would never have paid her the least bit of attention if they hadn't worked for the same agency. He'd told her more than once that she was beautiful, but she knew it was only because he felt obligated to do so and not because it was true. She'd been a bit on the heavy side growing up, and her schoolmates had teased her daily. So by the time she was a teenager, she'd lost all confidence in herself and in the way she looked.

But in terms of her feelings for Curtis, she'd actually liked him from the very beginning and had fallen in love with him right after their first date. He was strong, compassionate, tall, dark, and handsome, and from that point she started praying for their relationship to become serious. She prayed that God would give her Curtis even if it meant she had to go without something else in life. Whatever that had to be. So when he asked her to marry him, she knew for sure that God answered all prayers.

Mariah watched Curtis twirl his hands, demonstrating what he was saying.

"God will allow you to experience every twist and turn in the road until you are as strong as He needs you to be . . . until you are strong enough to deal with any trial or tribulation thrown your way," Curtis said. "And when it comes to success and prosperity, we have to take the same attitude. Sometimes we find ourselves climbing higher and higher in our chosen careers and all of a sudden a monkey wrench is thrown into the program. And of course, we as human beings don't understand it. We don't understand why God would give us such great success and then, for whatever reason, take us down a notch or two. But the best way I can explain it is to tell you what I heard on the radio last week. I was driving along, listening to 106.3, and it was then that I heard T.D. Jakes make one of the most profound statements. He said, 'A *setback* is a *setup* for a *comeback.*' "

"Oh, thank you, Jesus!" one woman stood and yelled out.

"Glory be to God!" another added with her hands lifted toward the ceiling.

"Boy, you know you workin' that Word on us today!" an older gentleman offered.

The organist played a few notes, and Mariah stood with her hands on both hips, waving her head from side to side with quick movements, giving Curtis approval. Then a woman jumped from her seat, shouting her way across three people sitting on the same row. This, of course, was all Curtis needed to see in order to switch into his deep southern preaching mode. He'd told Mariah that he thought it was totally ridiculous to sing the ending of every sermon, but that he'd learned during his days at Faith that his older members didn't feel like a pastor could preach if he didn't do a little whooping and singing with it. And since his older members were the major tithe and offering contributors, he gave them what they wanted.

"I saiddd, that Godd will allow a setback, which is a setup for a great comeback. I hearddd the bible say, we may endure for a night, but joyyy, I saiddd, joyyy will come in the morning," Curtis sang, and then broke out of the pulpit, sobbing and running around the full length of the church, hugging himself tightly. Mariah did the holy dance back and forth across the front of the church, and ten other people did the same thing up and down the center aisle. The spirit was moving frantically throughout the entire church, and continued for almost twenty minutes. Finally, everyone began settling down, and Curtis stood up from where he'd been kneeling and walked back into the pulpit.

"Oh, I tell you, the Holy Spirit is in here today, church," he announced while wiping sweat from his forehead and neck with a white Ralph Lauren bath towel. One of the women in the health unit had brought it over to him, and Mariah was glad they'd remembered to purchase a stack of them. Curtis had mentioned that the generic ones they'd been bringing him each Sunday were much too rough, and that he would much rather have something made by one of the top designers. That way, he wouldn't have to worry about the quality after they'd been washed a few times.

"There is nothing like a visit from the Lord," Curtis

continued. "There is nothing in this world that can compare to being in His presence."

"Amen," the congregation spoke in agreement.

Mariah was filled with so much joy that she wanted to burst wide open. She was sure that life could never be better than it was today.

I MMEDIATELY AFTER CHURCH, Curtis and Mariah had gone over to Deacon Taylor's house to have dinner with him and his family. Deacon Taylor was one of the deacons Curtis had appointed just before he lost his position at Faith. The deacon was very loyal to Curtis and dedicated to the church, and he was the primary reason Curtis was now pastor at Truth. He, along with the hundreds of Curtis's former members, had requested that Curtis be considered for the job.

Curtis and Mariah had spent three hours visiting with them and were now walking through the kitchen doorway of their own home. Usually they had afternoon or evening services to attend on Sundays, and Mariah was thankful that this was one of those rare instances when they didn't.

"Come here, you," Curtis said, grabbing Mariah playfully yet passionately.

Mariah always felt like melting whenever he pulled her into his arms. She felt so loved and so secure.

"Have I told you how much I love you?" she asked, gazing at him.

"No. Not today, anyway," he said, smiling.

"Well, I do, Curtis. I love you from the bottom of my soul, and all I want is to make you happy."

"Baby, you do make me happy. You've done that since the first day we started seeing each other."

"I really hope so, because I've heard so many women talking about how easy it is for a man to become bored with his wife. And I don't ever want you to feel that way. I want you to tell me if there is something wrong or if there is something I can do differently."

"Look, Mariah, I love you just the way you are. Believe me, I have no complaints."

Mariah sighed with relief.

Curtis removed her blazer and pecked her on the lips. Then he kissed her neck and her chest. Mariah moaned with every show of affection. Curtis unbuttoned her silk blouse, reached under it, and unsnapped her bra. He caressed her breasts roughly, kissing her at the same time.

"Do you want it here or upstairs?" he teased.

"Upstairs," she answered.

"No, I think we'd better take care of each other right here. Don't you?"

"No, sweetheart. Let's just go upstairs so we can be more comfortable," she said, pulling him close and kissing him.

"Okay, but first let me watch you undress the rest of the way."

Mariah always felt fat and uneasy whenever Curtis asked her to do this, but she went ahead and slipped off her blouse, bra, and skirt. Then she removed her nylon hose and panties and took a step toward him.

"No. Don't move. Just let me look at you. Let me look at what God created," he said, relaxing on the sofa and locking his hands behind his head.

"Curtis," she pleaded.

"What? Can I help it if I want to see all of you from head to toe? Because you really are beautiful. Your body is perfect."

"You know this embarrasses me," she told him. Not to mention she didn't think stripping like some nightclub dancer was something a pastor's wife should be doing, anyway.

"But why does it embarrass you?"

"Because it does."

"Well, you might as well get used to it, baby, because the main reason God created Eve was so she could pleasure Adam. So, satisfying your husband is part of your duty."

"I thought Eve was created so that Adam wouldn't be lonely, and so he would have a companion?" Mariah asked.

"Companionship, pleasure. Call it whatever you want, but it all means basically the same thing."

"I guess," she said, losing the mood because of all this conversation and because he was staring at her.

"Come here," he said, reaching his hand out to her. "I hate to say this, but I wasn't truthful with you earlier."

"You weren't truthful about what?" she asked, and sat

down next to him. She felt nervous and wondered what he was referring to.

"I wasn't being truthful when I said that I love you just the way you are, and that I have no complaints."

Mariah was speechless, because the last thing she wanted was for him to be dissatisfied with her.

"You still haven't given me oral sex, and that's something I'm used to getting. I know you said you didn't feel comfortable doing it because it seemed lustful and dirty. But the truth is, God doesn't have a problem with anything sexual as long as it's done between a man and his wife."

"I know you keep saying that, but I need more time, Curtis."

"How *much* more time, baby, because I've already given you six months. I mean, how much longer am I going to have to wait for something I've never had to go without?"

"I promise you I'm going to do it very soon."

"You don't seem to have a problem when I do it for you," he said matter-of-factly.

"But it's not like I ask you to do it or like it's required."

"But I can tell that you love it, and not once can I remember you turning it down."

Mariah didn't respond, because she knew he was right. She never, ever turned it down. But even though she enjoyed it, she still felt as though it was somehow unnatural and morally wrong. Especially since Curtis always turned into a ravenous animal whenever they arrived at that point of their lovemaking. He seemed to be obsessed with doing that to her, and it was almost as if he enjoyed it more than she did. But regardless, she just didn't feel comfortable doing it for him.

"Curtis, honey, I know you really want this, but I don't think it's right. I mean, why can't we make love to each other without doing all of that?"

"Because, I want more than just regular intercourse. I *need* so much more than that. And at some point you're going to have to get over this squeamish mentality," he said, turning his head away from her.

"I know, Curtis. And I promise you, I'm going to pray about this every day until God gives me the strength to do it."

"*Pray?*" he said, wrinkling his forehead. "As far as I'm concerned, there's nothing to pray about. Either you're going to do it or you're not. But I'm telling you, if I don't get it soon, I can't be responsible—"

"You can't be responsible for what?" she interrupted.

"Nothing. I didn't mean anything at all. And hey, why don't we just forget about making love altogether," he said, and stood up.

"Okay, Curtis. I'll do it."

"No, that's okay, because I don't want you doing something just for the sake of doing it."

"It won't be like that. I promise. I mean, I've never done anything like this before, but I'm willing to try."

Curtis removed every stitch of clothing he was wearing and stepped in front of her. "It won't be as bad as you think."

Mariah didn't know how she should respond, so she didn't.

"And, baby?" he said.

"Yes," she answered, wondering how she was going to get through this.

"I want you to know that even though I already love you more than anything in this world, I'll love you even more after tonight. I'll love you in a way that you can't even imagine. Our marriage will rise to a whole new level, because we will finally have bonded completely."

"I love you, too, Curtis," Mariah said, and realized that this truly was important to her husband, and that his love for her was all that really mattered. She decided that as his wife, it was her job to keep him happy.

It was her job to keep him faithful.

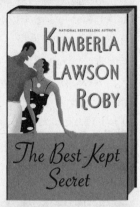
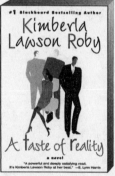